Against the Boards

Against the Boards

Lorna Schultz Nicholson

James Lorimer & Company Ltd., Publishers
Toronto

James Lorimer & Company Ltd. acknowledges the support of the Ontario Arts Council. We acknowledge the support of the Government of Canada through the Book Publishing Industry Development Program (BPIDP) for our publishing activities. We acknowledge the support of the Canada Council for the Arts for our publishing program. We acknowledge the support of the Government of Ontario through the Ontario Media Development Corporation's Ontario Book Initiative.

Cover illustration: Greg Ruhl

The Canada Council | Le Conseil des Arts
for the Arts | du Canada

ONTARIO ARTS COUNCIL
CONSEIL DES ARTS DE L'ONTARIO

National Library of Canada Cataloguing in Publication

Schultz Nicholson, Lorna
   Against the Boards / Lorna Schultz Nicholson.

(Sports stories ; 77)
ISBN 1-55028-865-2 (bound).   ISBN 1-55028-864-4 (pbk.)

I. Title. II. Series: Sports stories (Toronto, Ont.); 77.

PS8637.C49A32 2005   jC813'.6   C2005-900228-X

James Lorimer & Company Ltd.,
Publishers
35 Britain Street
Toronto, Ontario
M5A 1R7
www.lorimer.ca

Distributed in the United States by:
Orca Book Publishers
P.O. Box 468
Custer, WA USA
98240-0468

Printed and bound in Canada.

Contents

Acknowledgments

Thank you to all my readers for telling me to "hurry up and write another book." I love it when you children tell me your thoughts and feelings about my work — it makes every word worth the effort. Thank you Jordon Tootoo, you are an inspiration to so many young players. And a huge thank you goes to Wayne Gretzky and Pat Quinn for their quotes. I feel honoured by these hockey legends — they are true team players. And, of course, it does take a team to make a book-so thanks to the editorial team at Lorimer. Now, enjoy everyone.

To Dad
I miss you

1

Tryouts

Peter Kuiksak gripped the plastic handle of his brand new black hockey bag and wheeled it into the dressing room. His hands were clammy with sweat, and his stomach rolled like a big wave. *Tryouts*.

He'd never had to go through this before because where he was from — Tuktoyaktuk, North West Territories — they barely had enough kids to make a team. Why had he agreed to fly all the way to Edmonton to try out for this Bantam team?

The eerie quiet of the dressing room — even though it was packed with players — made Peter's stomach feel even worse. Right beside the door, he saw an available seat. He plunked his bag down and squished himself in between two guys. Without saying a word, he tugged open the zipper.

He leaned over, silently reminding himself of the reason why he was in Edmonton in this hot dressing room feeling like he couldn't breathe. This was his big chance to become a better hockey player. Spending part of his summer at an elite hockey camp, he had seen kids play hockey at a level he had only imagined before. Now he desperately wanted to improve and see if one day he could actually become an NHL hockey player, like Jordin Tootoo. He knew his only hope of doing that was to move away from the Arctic to somewhere he could train with better players.

He sucked in a deep breath and pulled out his socks and shinpads. Neither guy beside him spoke a word. Just as well. Peter didn't feel like talking to anyone.

Within ten minutes, he was dressed — record speed for sure. He snapped on his helmet so no one could see his face ... and the sweat dripping off his brow. Would he be able to keep up?

Peter jiggled his leg. He leaned against the wall, then leaned forward, then leaned back again. He couldn't get comfortable, and his horrible stomach cramps wouldn't go away. The dressing room was so packed he had to sit shoulder-to-shoulder with the guys on either side of him. No one talked.

Finally, after what felt to Peter like hours of sitting under the blazing summer sun, the door opened and a man walked in wearing a track jacket with "Sherwood Park AAA Bantam" emblazoned on it. The man explained the tryout procedure to the still super-quiet dressing room. Peter was assigned number thirty-two. He couldn't think of any way that it could be his lucky number. It wasn't his birthday, his dad's birthday, or his age. He pulled the practice jersey over his head and stepped onto the ice.

The first drill was skating. Peter lined up at the end zone, his legs shaking. He had to explode right from the start. The whistle blew. He dug in his edges, took off, and ... caught an edge.

After losing crucial moments regaining his balance, Peter pumped his legs, stopping and starting at every line. But there was no way he could catch up, and he ended up in the middle of the pack. Peter wasn't used to losing. Ever. In the Arctic, he could skate circles around *everybody*.

Peter was thankful when the skating drills were over. He slugged back some water before finding a spot on the bench. They'd divided everyone up and there were twenty-five guys to a team. With so many guys trying out, no player would see much ice time, so every shift had to count.

Peter heard his number and position called and quickly headed to right wing. He lined up, looked around to memorize his teammates, then lowered his head to concentrate on the face-off. The puck dropped and rolled, and he found himself in the middle of a scramble. He batted at the puck but couldn't get it, and a player from the other team picked it up. Peter skated after him. Once he was next to him, Peter bumped him hard into the boards. The guy lost his balance but somehow managed to pass the puck to one of his teammates, who took a shot on net. Peter's goalie threw up his glove hand and made a spectacular save.

Peter shook his head. His first shift out and the other team had managed a shot on net. He groaned. He'd played lousy.

After the ice session he quickly undressed, skipped the shower, and met his dad in front of the arena. They had to stay in a hotel room while Peter was at the tryouts. And rent a car. Peter knew this was costing his dad a lot of money. "I sucked," he grumbled.

There was no way Peter would ever make the NHL playing this way. His dreams of earning big bucks to help his dad had been squashed in one night.

His father patted him on the back. "No, you didn't. Give it some time. Tomorrow will be better. Come on, we'll head back to the hotel for some grub and a shower."

Peter didn't want to go back to a hotel room — he wanted to go home.

* * *

The first cut went up after the third tryout. Peter stood at the back of the crowd of jostling kids, searching for his name. When he saw it, he blew out a rush of air.

"Dad, I made the first cut," he said excitedly, rushing up to his dad in the lobby arena.

Mr. Kuiksak tousled Peter's hair. "Good for you. Now you just have to play the two exhibition games. Tomorrow is an inter-squad game."

Peter nodded. "Only thirty made it today so tomorrow, when they cut down to twenty-two guys, with fifteen on the bench, I'll get lots of ice. If I make it tomorrow, then the next day I play a real exhibition game against another Bantam team." He paused. "Do you think I'll make the team?"

"If you keep playing hard, you should."

"But ... who will I live with if I make it?" Peter asked quietly.

Mr. Kuiksak put his arm around him. "One step at a time, okay? Let's get through tomorrow's game and see what happens."

* * *

Peter had never been so nervous in his whole life. By the time the warm-up was over, his gloves were soaked and smelled like wet leather. He skated to the bench, gulped down some water, and waited for the coach to call out the lines.

First shift out on left wing, Peter body-checked a guy along the boards so hard the glass rattled. He knew it had been a good hit. So far, so good.

Second shift, as he jumped from the bench onto the ice, he intercepted a pass. He took off, and a player from the other team chased him. Peter managed to stay one step ahead. Then two steps ahead.

He had a breakaway.

Here was his chance! As he reached the goalie, he wondered what he should do — shoot or deke? The goalie moved forward, playing out of his net, and Peter could see that he had one entire side of the net covered. In a split second, Peter decided to deke. He faked a shot, then toed his stick to flip the puck over to the side. The goalie poked at the puck but couldn't reach it. Peter ripped the puck into the open side of the net!

His team won the game 5–4, and Peter scored two of the five goals.

After the game, Peter raced out of the dressing room. At the end of the hallway, where the list was posted, he saw his father deep in conversation with the head coach of the Sherwood Park team and a man and a woman. Peter slowed his steps. Why was his father talking to the coach? Who were those other people?

Some of the other guys were already standing by the bulletin board, looking for their names. Was the coach telling his dad they should go home now? Peter sucked in a deep breath. He wanted to throw up.

He inched toward the board. One guy passed him, crying. Another guy hit his stick against the concrete arena wall. Two other guys cheered and high-fived each other.

Peter scanned down the list ... he saw his name! Excited, he waved to his father, who motioned him to come over.

"Congratulations, Peter," said the coach.

"Thanks," said Peter shyly. It was weird actually talking to the coach. And his dad was being really quiet.

"You can call me Coach John." He smiled. "I'd like to introduce you to Mr. and Mrs. Patterson."

Peter held out his hand, embarrassed that it smelled of wet leather. "Hi," was all he could manage to say.

"The Pattersons have requested that you live with them this year while you play for the Sherwood Park Arrows. Their son, Trevor, is playing on a Major Junior team in Red Deer.

"But ... what about tomorrow? Isn't there another tryout, another game?" Peter was confused.

"Tomorrow is for the bubble kids," said Coach John. "You don't have to prove anything more to us. You're solid."

"Coach John figures we'll need the time to get you home and packed," said Peter's dad.

"You mean ... I made the team?" Peter stared wide-eyed at the coach.

"Coach John has already helped us get our flight changed, Peter. We'll leave tonight," said his dad.

"And I've already got someone looking into your return flight," said Coach John. "We need you here by the end of the week for practice and for the first day of school."

"I'll make sure to go to the school tomorrow to register you, Peter," said Mrs. Patterson, smiling. "I think some of the boys on the team will be at your junior high."

Coach John patted Peter's back. "You'll be a tremendous asset to this team, Peter. I'm looking forward to a good year."

When Peter looked at his dad, he tried to smile but he couldn't. Everything was happening so fast. Up until this moment, it had all been just a pipe dream. Now ... it was reality.

He had to move away from home.

2

Leaving Tuk

"You're so lucky, Peter, that you get to move away from here." Peter's friend Mike slapped him on the back.

They stood by the water's edge beside Peter's packed bags. Lots of people had come to the Arctic shore to see Peter off — his Auntie (who had helped so much after his mother had died), his little brothers and sisters, his cousins, his big sister Susie and his new little niece, and lots of his friends.

Peter's news about making the Edmonton AAA team had spread through the little hamlet of Tuktoyaktuk in minutes. By the time Peter had arrived home with his dad, everyone knew. He couldn't walk down the street without someone coming up and congratulating him. Now so many had come to say good-bye. Overnight, he had become the hamlet hero.

If he was so lucky why did he feel so funny? "Yeah, I guess," he shrugged when he realized Mike was waiting for an answer.

"What do you mean, you guess?" Another friend, Jason, jabbed his shoulder. "Beats pumping gas. Just think of all the girls you'll meet. And no more ice roads. Who knows — maybe you'll become a big star!"

"You think so?" Peter hoisted his hockey bag into the motor boat. Until the cold set in, the only way to travel out of

Tuktoyaktuk was by boat. Once the water froze, they could go by ice road, but winter was still a few months away. The motor boat chugged and gas fumes clouded the air.

"Think! I know you can do it." Mike smiled and nodded his head.

Peter tried to smile back. Tuk was so small that everyone knew everyone. These guys had been his friends since he was little. They'd all played hockey together and drum danced, dog raced and kayaked. All summer long they rode their bikes and played pick-up ball late into the night. In the North, the sun never set in the summer, so everyone was up all night long. Sometimes they even played baseball at two in the morning. He looked out into the distance toward the horizon line, seeing nothing but ocean water. The North Pole was close.

He thought about how, in the winter, he would snowmobile with Mike and Jason way out onto the frozen ocean. They'd do donuts and make jumps when they were supposed to be hunting. Peter turned away from the ocean to look back at his little hamlet. Most of the houses sat perched on stilts because, with the ground always frozen, you couldn't dig more than a foot below the surface. And they were all pretty small — one floor with a kitchen, living room, bathroom, and two bedrooms. What would his new house be like?

In the winter, he could snowmobile from one end of Tuk to the other in five minutes. They all drove snowmobiles to the arenas. On game day, there'd be twenty of them lined up outside like cars. Guaranteed, he wouldn't be snowmobiling to his games in Edmonton. He was moving to a big city; a really big city. Peter's stomach flip-flopped.

He'd never lived anywhere but the Arctic.

His sister Susie stepped forward. Her baby, Lisa, born while Peter had been away at hockey camp, was snuggled in a papoose. Just two years older than Peter, Susie was one of his best friends. Susie and Peter used to harpoon fish all summer long, and in the winter they were on the same drum dancing team. Some of the guys at hockey camp seemed shocked to hear that Peter's sister was a mother at fifteen, but Peter had explained that, in the North, lots of teenage girls had babies. Now Susie took care of Lisa and worked as a cashier at the Northern Store. She was lucky to have such a good job.

Like all of Peter's brothers and sisters, Susie always came to Peter's games — she was his biggest fan. Tilting her head, she smiled at Peter. "Are you coming home for winter solstice?"

He touched baby Lisa's soft fuzzy scalp. "If we don't have a tournament or something like that, I can try. It costs lots to fly, though."

"Lisa will have grown a lot by then. Maybe she'll even be sitting up."

He nodded. "Maybe you and Dad and Lisa can come down to Edmonton. Lisa can go on the plane for free."

"I don't know about that." Susie shook her head. She had never been further than Yellowknife, for shopping. There were no big stores in Tuk. In fact, Tuk was so small there was just the Northern Store, which had everything from groceries to clothes to plastic toys.

"I've heard they have a mall that's the biggest in the world," said Peter.

"You'll do good, Peter. You're going to make us all so proud."

The rest of his brothers and sisters came to surround him and Susie. Peter felt a lump form in his throat and he turned away from his family and friends. Everyone was counting on him to be the next northern star. What if he couldn't live up to their hopes?

He felt a hand on his shoulder. "Come on, Pete. We should get going. We have a long boat ride ahead of us, and a flight with some stops."

Peter nodded. "Bye, Susie." He rubbed his nose to hers in an old Inuit gesture. He hugged all his siblings and told Jeremy, the next oldest boy, to make sure he helped Dad out.

Then he jumped into the boat.

"Knock 'em dead, Peter."

As the boat chugged forward, Peter waved to everyone on the shore. Then his father gunned it and they were cruising at high speed. The people in the distance got smaller and smaller.

When they were around the first bend, Peter sat forward, pulled his hoodie over his head, and sighed. This was it. He was moving from Tuktoyaktuk to Edmonton to play hockey.

3

New Home

The boat ride took four hours. Then they had to wait in the Inuvik airport for an hour for their flight. Finally, Peter walked across the tarmac to board the plane. The drone of the plane's engine helped drown out his thoughts. But when he sat in his seat and snapped up his seat belt, he had to close his eyes and lean back. He really was leaving.

The plane landed in Yellowknife and they had a forty-five minute wait there. Peter bought a Coke and a magazine in the one airport store. His father bought a coffee. They talked a bit about the Edmonton Oilers and how they were going to have a good team this year.

The next flight took off on time, and Peter actually managed to sleep for an hour or so. Finally, at around seven in the evening, he glanced out the small window to see the sprawling city of Edmonton — houses, roads, warehouses, sports fields. The downtown buildings stood tall, even though they looked like toy blocks from the plane. Peter had flown to Edmonton for the tryouts, but he was still shocked at the size of the city. He gripped the side of his seat.

"You'll be fine, Pete," said his dad, patting his hand.

He stiffly leaned back and squeezed his eyes shut.

"It might take some adjusting, but you'll be okay," continued his dad. "This is your big chance."

"I know."

"You're going to have to really work on your school work, too. Your coach told me all his players have to keep their marks up to play on his team."

Peter opened his eyes and played with the ties on his hoodie. "What if ... I can't keep up? School's different in the city, Dad."

"I'll talk to your coach and get someone to help you."

"Don't do that, Dad. Please."

"There's nothing wrong with getting a little help now and again."

Peter slouched in his seat. "I won't need help."

"What do you call those people who help kids with their homework?"

"You mean tutors?"

"Yeah," said his dad. "If you need help, we'll get one of those for you."

"No way," said Peter. "I told you I'd be okay. Anyway, they're not cheap, you know.

Mr. Kuiksak leaned forward and peered out the window. "The Pattersons wanted to pick us up, but I rented a car."

Even though Peter's dad had a government job working for the Hamlet of Tuktoyaktuk, Peter knew the trip was costing his dad money he didn't really have.

* * *

After making two wrong turns, Mr. Kuiksak finally found the street they were looking for. He drove slowly so Peter could read the numbers.

"Do they know we're coming tonight?" Peter asked, staring

out the window at the houses. "If they don't, we could just get that hotel again."

"I talked to them before we left."

"All the houses are so big!"

"You'll have your own room. At least, that's what they said." Peter's dad slowed the car to a crawl. "Here we are. Number sixteen." He stopped the car and turned off the engine.

Peter tapped his fingers on his jeans and jiggled his foot. "Why don't we go to that hotel tonight? That one we stayed at during tryouts? It was okay for the money, wasn't it?"

His dad seemed to read his mind. "Pete, I'm staying here tonight, too. My flight doesn't leave until after practice tomorrow morning."

"Okay." Peter paused before he stepped outside onto the curb.

Mr. and Mrs. Patterson opened the front door when Peter and his dad were only halfway up the walk.

"Hello, Peter. We've been waiting for you." Mrs. Patterson held the door wide open. She wore a big smile.

Peter continued up the walk, sticking close to his father.

"Are you hungry?" Mrs. Patterson asked when Peter had mounted the front stairs. She patted him gently on the shoulder. "We saved dinner."

Peter tried to smile, but his mouth wouldn't move. And he couldn't speak. His tongue seemed to be stuck to the roof of his mouth.

The Pattersons ushered Peter into the house. Standing in the front entrance, Peter gasped. The entrance alone was as big as the kitchen back home.

Off to the left side was a room that had shiny new-looking furniture. Nothing seemed out of place. The Pattersons had lots of glass stuff, vases full of flowers, and a big cabinet filled with all kinds of plates and wine glasses. The room looked as if no one ever went in it. And it had carpet.

At his house they had an old green sofa, a kitchen table with a broken leg, and no carpet. His father hadn't gotten around to putting down flooring after putting together their house. All the pieces for the house had come in big boxes from the south. They were called do-it-yourself houses. Susie cleaned up all the time and tried to make things nice by putting a fancy tablecloth on for meals. She always complained that none of the rest of the family cared about what she did. Susie would think *this* house was "to die for." It was her favourite saying.

Further down the hall on the same side was another room. Then across the hall more rooms! A young boy with blond hair eating an apple walked into the hallway. Did he just come from the kitchen?

"Andrew, meet Peter." Mrs. Patterson grinned at Peter. "He's been waiting for you. Since Trevor left, he doesn't have anyone to play mini-sticks with."

"Hi," said Andrew. He wiped the juice from the apple off his mouth and grinned. "Do you really live near the North Pole?"

"Yeah," mumbled Peter.

"Wow, that's cool."

"Andrew, why don't you take Peter up to his room? Then you can show him the rest of the house." Again, Mrs. Patterson smiled at Peter, enough to show almost all her teeth. They were so white. Dentists came only once in a while to Tuk and lots of Peter's relatives had black teeth.

"We have a daughter, too," she continued. "She's going into grade nine, so she's one year older than you." Mrs. Patterson looked at her watch. "She should be home soon."

"You can sleep in our son Trevor's room for tonight," said

Mr. Patterson to Peter's dad. He turned to Andrew. "Show Mr. Kuiksak to Trevor's room, too. Okay, bud?"

"Sure," said Andrew.

"Then come on down to the kitchen, both of you. I'll fix you up a plate of food. You must be starving after a long day of travelling. They don't feed you on those small planes." Mrs. Patterson pointed in the direction the boy had come from. "The kitchen is through that door."

"Thank you," said Peter's dad.

Peter just nodded.

When Peter entered his bedroom, his eyes widened. He had a double bed, a dresser, a little table, and ... a phone. Did all kids have phones in their rooms in the city? "You can put your clothes in here." Andrew opened the closet door. "We cleaned it all out. You should have seen the junk in there. What a mess."

The clothes Peter brought would fill maybe one quarter of the closet.

"Wait till you meet my sister. She's a pain," said Andrew. "She thinks she's *so cool* 'cause she's going into *grade nine*. Whooppee. You guys are at the same junior high. She sleeps in the basement now 'cause she *wanted a bigger room* and she wanted to be closer to the *computer* so she can chat with her friends. Now, I never get on the computer 'cause she hogs it all the time."

Unzipping his bag, Peter pulled out the new blue pants and white shirt his dad had bought for him. Coach John said Peter needed nice pants, a dress shirt, and a tie for games. He took a hanger off the rod and hung up his pants and shirt. They looked funny all by themselves in such a big closet.

"I'm going downstairs," said Andrew. "When you're done, I'll show you the rest of the house."

"Sure," said Peter, suddenly realizing that it was the first word he'd said since he'd entered his new room.

4

Christine

In less than five minutes, Peter had unpacked everything in his bag. He'd put clothes in two of the dresser drawers. Three drawers and well over half the closet remained empty. On the dresser, he placed the few pictures he had brought: one of Susie and baby Lisa, one of him and his friends down by the Lady of Lourdes ship in Tuk, and one of Josh Watson and him at hockey camp. Josh had been his roommate and they had had a great time, becoming good friends by the end of the week. Since camp had ended in early July, they had been e-mailing each other all the time. He wished Josh lived in Edmonton instead of Calgary. At least then he'd have one friend here.

How was he to talk to Josh now? Plus all his friends up in Tuk? He'd promised them he'd stay in touch.

He carefully placed his drum on the floor in the closet. It was just a small drum, but it was portable. The bigger drums at home would have been hard to take on the plane, especially with his hockey gear. This one he had made at school, in art class. Would he ever get to use it, or would they think it was weird? He closed the closet doors.

As he headed back downstairs, he heard his dad's voice. He sighed in relief. He didn't want to walk all by himself into a kitchen full of people he didn't know.

Peter trod quietly down the hall and was about to turn toward the kitchen when the front door banged open. A girl with long brown hair bounced into the house. After she threw the bag she was carrying over her shoulder onto the floor, she slipped out of her skater shoes. She wore tight jeans and a T-shirt with "Billabong" written across the front. Peter recognized the brand name because it was all Susie talked about. Billabong wasn't in any of the catalogues she ordered clothes from and it drove her crazy because she wanted one of their hoodies so badly.

Suddenly, Peter realized he was standing frozen to the spot. He needed to get into the kitchen fast! He didn't want this girl to see him staring. She looked up. Too late.

"Uh-oh. You must be Peter. That means I'm late," she said, grimacing.

Again, his tongue seemed to be stuck somewhere in the top of his mouth.

"When did you get here?" She whispered, scrunching up her face.

He knew he had to answer her. "Um, I dunno. Fifteen minutes ago."

"So, I'm not really late then," she replied.

He shrugged. How was he to know if she was late?

"Christine, is that you?" Mrs. Patterson came out from the kitchen. She raised her eyebrows. "I told you to be home by nine."

"I know, Mom, but we just got so busy. We had to splice the tape, and that took forever. You should see our routine though. Madison and I are singing, and Jemma and Gillian made up this great dance to go with our singing. I think we'll wow them." She even bounced when she talked, flinging her hair all over the place.

Mrs. Patterson turned to Peter. "Christine and her friends

are opening the Sherwood Park Junior High assembly on the first day of school." She smiled and turned back to Christine. "Did you meet Peter?" Mrs. Patterson placed her hand on Peter's shoulder.

"Yeah, we met."

"You'll have to show him around the school. Introduce him to everyone."

"*He's in grade eight, Mom.* I don't know any of those kids."

"Well then, you can introduce him to kids on the bus." Mrs. Patterson smiled at Peter, but he felt like crawling under a rock. How embarrassing. This girl didn't want to show him around the school. And Peter didn't want her to, anyway.

"Come on, Peter," said Mrs. Patterson. "I've got some dinner for you."

Peter ate his spaghetti in silence. Christine made an appearance in the kitchen, politely said hello to Mr. Kuiksak, grabbed a juice box and a few cookies, then bounced out of the kitchen to go to her room. She left saying something about getting her clothes and books ready for the first day of school. They still had one day left before school even started. Did all city kids get ready for school early? Did Christine ever just walk normal? Maybe all city girls were like her.

Andrew rolled his eyes and stuck out his tongue at her when she left. Then he leaned over and said to Peter, "Told you she thought she was cool,"

Peter lowered his head and kept shovelling food into his mouth. He liked the garlic bread. Good thing the food was okay. He wondered if he'd ever get to eat caribou here. Everyone ate caribou in Tuk. And muktuk. Muktuk was whale blubber, and all the kids ate it as if it was candy.

His dad made small talk with Mr. Patterson, but Peter knew by the grunted out words that he was uncomfortable, too. Once they finished eating, Andrew said he'd show Peter around the house. Peter really wanted to hide in his room with the door shut. Or go back to the hotel he stayed in last time with just his dad.

Downstairs proved to be Peter's biggest shock. The basement room was probably the size of Peter's whole house, including the porch. A big-screen television stood against the wall right in front of a big comfy-looking sofa, two bean-bag chairs, and another leather sofa. Peter noticed the computer on a desk in the corner. A big bookshelf, full of tons of books, loomed beside the desk. Peter had never seen so many books. There were more books here than in the library in Tuk. He continued scanning the room … and stopped when he saw the other corner. Thrown haphazardly on the floor were mini-sticks, next to a mini-stick net, and … an air-hockey game!

"You want a game?" Andrew asked, pointing to the game. He must have seen the surprised look on Peter's face.

"Yeah, sure. Okay." They had an air-hockey game at the Tuk community centre, but no one had one in their *house*.

They ran over and Andrew turned it on. Peter immediately heard the familiar hissing of the air.

They batted the small plastic puck back and forth, back and forth. Peter scored, then Andrew scored. Then Peter went up by two. He became so immersed in the game, it was only when Mrs. Patterson called from upstairs to tell them it was time for bed that he realized Christine was in the room with them, sitting at the computer. Andrew scored when Peter became distracted.

"We should go up now," said Peter, putting the round paddle on the air-hockey table.

"We have a few more minutes before she calls down again," said Andrew. "Come on. Give me a chance to redeem myself. I'm only one goal down now."

Peter wasn't sure what to do. At home, he stayed up late all the time. No one ever told him to go to bed, especially not a mother. But this was his first night in this house and he should listen to Mrs. Patterson. Would she think he was bad if he didn't? On the other hand, if he suddenly stopped playing and went upstairs, Andrew might get mad at him. Maybe if he didn't play too hard and let Andrew have a few more goals, then the game would be over. Everyone would be happy.

The air-hockey puck went back and forth a few times before Peter let it slide past his goalie. Andrew jumped up and down, punching his fists in the air.

"Do you have to yell so loud?" Christine glared at Andrew. "Mom said it was time for bed, you know."

"So?"

"I think I'm going to go upstairs," said Peter. "I've got early morning practice. Good game, Andrew." Peter placed his air-hockey puck and paddle in the middle of the table as Andrew pressed the switch to turn the game off.

"Let's have a rubber match tomorrow. It's our last day of summer holidays, then, yuk, we have to go back to school. You have to go to school with *her.*" Andrew swiped at Christine's hair when he walked by her.

"Cut it out, you little jerk."

"Who are you talking to — your boyfriend?"

"None of your business. Go upstairs."

Not sure if she was talking to him, too, Peter didn't want to stick around to find out. Anyway, he wanted to see his dad before he went to bed. Practice was at nine in the morning, and then his dad was leaving from the arena to go back out to the airport.

After saying good-night to everyone, Peter went into his new bedroom and shut the door. He flopped down on his new bed and lay on his back, staring at the ceiling. It felt so weird being in a strange house with strange people, and being in a room all alone. At home, he and his brothers all slept in one room. He wished he could hear their breathing or one of them coughing. The silence made it hard to sleep. What would tomorrow be like when his father was gone?

And what would it be like going to school that first day?

* * *

Peter awoke at six o'clock, but didn't want to go downstairs until he heard someone else up, so he lay on his bed, staring at the clock. The minutes ticked by. Peter had set the alarm to go off at seven, in time for him to have some breakfast and get to practice. Peter watched the little red numbers on the clock change. Coach wanted everyone there forty-five minutes early for practices and an hour and a half before games. At home, Peter arrived fifteen minutes ahead for both practices and games.

When the numbers read 6:59, Peter shut the alarm off. He was getting dressed when he heard a rap on his door.

"Peter," said Mrs. Patterson, almost singing his name. "Are you up?"

"Yeah," Peter mumbled. Was she going to knock on his door every morning? At home, Peter didn't even have a bedroom door. Peter slipped on his jeans and a T-shirt, then looked in the mirror. What if his clothes weren't cool enough?

Quietly, he opened the door of his room and tiptoed into the hall. Was his father awake? Should he knock on his door? Peter scanned the hall. Was anyone in the bathroom? The door was shut. He stood in the hall and listened for sounds — water running or a toilet flushing. Hearing nothing, he edged toward the door. Suddenly, the door creaked a bit. He jumped back and hurried toward the stairs. He couldn't get caught lurking by the bathroom door.

"Hey, Pete," he heard his dad whisper.

Peter breathed in relief. "Dad," he said, turning. "Are you done in there? I gotta go."

His dad nodded. "I talked with the Pattersons last night after you went to bed. You have to get some books today for school tomorrow. They said they would help. I don't want to change my flight, so they said they would take you shopping so I can still head out right after practice. Is that okay?"

"Yeah, I guess."

"They're real nice people."

Peter nodded. His father walked toward him and patted him on the back. "I'm looking forward to seeing you practise this morning."

"Yeah, it should be good," said Peter.

If only he believed his own words.

5

First Practice

Music blared from the dressing room. Peter shoved open the door and walked into a room full of guys talking, laughing, and horsing around. When he saw an available spot by the goalie, he manoeuvred around all the equipment and sat down.

"Hi," said the goalie. "My name's Stu."

"Hi," replied Peter, leaning over to unzip his bag.

"You're the kid from the North, right?"

"Yeah."

"Cool." A wad of tape smacked Stu on the side of the head. He stood up and chucked the tape back.

The guy on the other side seemed just as quiet as Peter. Good, thought Peter, he didn't want to talk anyway.

Peter was dressed and ready for practice within ten minutes. Now he had to sit and wait. He wasn't nervous like he was at tryouts. After all, he'd made the team without even playing the final game. That must mean he was pretty good — in the top half at least. But he still felt weird, as if he didn't fit in. He was thankful when the coach finally pushed open the door and walked in.

"Congratulations to each and every one of you," he said. "I know this is going to be a great team. My name is John Spence, but you can call me Coach John. I want to introduce you to my assistant coaches, Coach Phil and Coach Dave. " Both of the men wore "Sherwood Park AAA Bantam" track suits and already had their skates and hockey gloves on. They rested their chins on the tops of their sticks and lifted their hands to wave to the guys. The whole team cheered but Peter and the kid sitting beside him.

Three coaches! Up north, they only had one coach. Most of the time Peter ran the practices, and all they did was fool around and scrimmage.

Then Coach John pointed to another man who wasn't wearing skates but had a track suit on. "And meet Mr. Calver, our team manager. He's taken his first-aid course, so he will double as a trainer."

Manager? Trainer? Peter couldn't believe how many people were involved with this team.

"I've scheduled three practices this week. Then next Saturday, I've set up an exhibition game."

Most of the guys made cheering noises.

"Who are we playing, Coach John?" asked Stu when things had quieted down.

"Leduc. They'll be good. Okay, listen up. If you're going to play on my team, there are three main rules." He paused and glanced at every player. Then he said in a stern voice, "Number one — I want you here on time. And I mean to the minute. If you are late, you have the choice to either bag skate or miss the next game." He paused for a second to look around the room.

Peter had no idea what Coach John meant by "bag" skate, but he wasn't going to ask and look stupid.

Coach John continued. "Number two — you have to keep your marks up. I will be checking regularly with each one of your teachers. You slip, you don't play." Some of the players groaned.

"I'm serious, guys." He raised his eyebrows. "All right, number three. I do not tolerate stupid penalties. I will bench anyone who takes continuous bad penalties."

The only rule of the three that made Peter nervous was the school rule. School started the very next day. Peter didn't want to think about it. Today, he wanted to concentrate on hockey. That's why he was here, to play hockey.

After the players warmed up, skating fast and slow laps and stretching, the coach blew the whistle. Peter hustled to the circle. Everyone got down on one knee, including Peter, even though they never had to do that in Tuk. The coach pulled out the white board and started explaining the drill, the Crossover Snake. It was not one Peter had seen at summer camp, but he studied the board, hoping he had it figured out.

Explanations finished, Coach John blew the whistle and everyone quickly skated to the end zone. Peter followed. Somehow he ended up first in the line.

"Peter and Tanner, are you ready?" Coach John yelled.

Peter heard the whistle and took off to the first cone, making a tight turn. Suddenly, he heard a second whistle.

"Peter," Coach John yelled. "I said go around the cones in crossovers, not tight turns. And I want no forward striding once you hit that first cone. This is a drill for quick feet, so I want crossovers."

Peter flushed under his helmet.

"Go back, both of you. Peter, go to the back of the line and watch. Marc, you go first instead."

Lowering his head and batting at the snow on the ice with his stick, Peter skated to the back of the line. He felt like an idiot. The guy who sat beside him in the dressing room turned to him in the line.

"I've never done this drill, either," he whispered. "Must be one Coach John made up, and only guys who've played with him would know."

Peter ignored the boy and turned his attention to the guys performing the drill. Carefully, he watched every move they made. By the time it was his turn, he gritted his teeth in determination. When he heard the whistle, he took off like he'd never taken off before. He circled around the cones, moving his feet in continuous crossovers, almost as if he was skipping, and he almost caught up to Greg, who was in front of him.

Peter skated back feeling a little better.

Fortunately, the next drill — Net Drive — was one Peter had done at summer camp. He lined up at centre ice. Who was he paired with? He saw that he was with the quiet guy who sat beside him in the dressing room. Peter didn't know his name.

Peter heard the whistle, made a bounce pass off the boards, picked up the puck, and drove to the outside around two pylons. His partner pivoted at the first pylon then skated backwards between the pylons, trying to push Peter deep into the corner. But Peter wouldn't be pushed off the puck. He continued his outside drive and fired the puck with a wrist shot. Stu stuck out his glove and made an amazing glove save.

As Peter skated around the back of the net, heading back to the start position at centre ice, he wondered if he should say "good save" to Stu. Did the guys on this team do that, or was it just a given that the goalie would make the save? Without saying anything, Peter skated back to the line.

The rest of the practice flew by, and Peter couldn't believe it when he heard the Zamboni, the signal that it was time to hit the showers. In the dressing room, Peter's stomach churned when the guys starting talking about school.

Peter didn't want to start school tomorrow. Why couldn't he just live in Edmonton and play hockey?

6

School

Peter awoke before his alarm. When he sat up, his stomach did major somersaults. He ran to the bathroom, quickly shut the door, and threw up in the toilet. Then he glanced around the bathroom. He couldn't wipe his mouth on the green towel — someone might smell that he'd thrown up. What about toilet paper? He ripped some off the roll, cleaned himself up, flushed the toilet, and reached for his tooth brush. What if he had to throw up at school?

Back in his room, Peter picked up the books the Pattersons had helped him pick out. That Staples store had been three times the size of the community hall at home. They carried everything from desks to computers to ... school supplies. He put his books down and picked up the lock they had also bought. The day before he'd spent an hour trying the lock combination.

Christine had told him that Sherwood Park Junior High School had more than five hundred kids for just grades seven through nine. His entire hamlet of Tuk — adults and kids — was only a thousand people! The school he had to go to today was over half the size of Tuk. Peter closed his eyes, willing himself not to throw up again.

Mangilaluk School in Tuk had around three hundred kids, but it went from kindergarten to grade twelve. What would it be like attending a school where all the kids were his age?

He packed his books into his new backpack. What was he supposed to do now? Mrs. Patterson had told him where to find towels. He should have a shower. Or would he wake everyone up?

Peter sat down on his bed and rocked back and forth, hoping this would help settle his stomach. Ten minutes later, he heard the rap on his door.

"Peter, time to get up." Was Mrs. Patterson going to knock on his door every morning?

"I'm up," he said.

"Remember, if you want a shower there are towels in the linen closet in the hallway."

"Okay," replied Peter. He definitely needed a shower to get rid of the puke smell.

After his shower, Peter dressed in a T-shirt and jeans that he'd ordered from the Sears catalogue. He glanced in the mirror. What did the kids wear to school in the city? Today he'd find out. Blowing out a huge rush of air, Peter picked up his bag. It weighed a ton!

Downstairs, he found Mrs. Patterson busy in the kitchen.

"I've made some eggs. You need a good breakfast today." No one had ever made breakfast for Peter. Sometimes Susie tried, but not very often. They ate cereal or Pop-Tarts or sometimes just muktuk if a whale had been harpooned.

"And I've got your lunch made, too." Holding a spatula in her hand, Mrs. Patterson pointed to the kitchen counter. "That one on the end is yours. I figure you'll eat more than Christine."

"What are you saying about me?" Christine walked into the kitchen. She wore a short pink skirt with a pink T-shirt. She threw her backpack on the ground. "Mother, I am not taking a lunch kit." She swung open the door below the sink and pulled out a white plastic grocery bag. She scanned the lunches, picking the one she obviously knew was hers, and threw all the stuff in the bag. Then she shoved it into her backpack.

"Is that skirt long enough for school policy?" Mrs. Patterson raised her eyebrows.

Defiantly, Christine put her arms straight down to her sides and said, "Look, it goes down to my fingertips, and that's the dumb school rule."

"O-kay," said Mrs. Patterson. "Just checking. I want no phone calls home this year about your inappropriate dress.

Peter's mind was racing. Did they have rules for the boys too? He wondered why Christine didn't want to take a lunch kit. Was that not a cool thing to do? Peter had never taken a lunch to school. Tuk was so small they all went home or to the bakery or coffee shop. Was he supposed to eat with kids he didn't know?

"Peter, did you want a lunch kit?" Mrs. Patterson's voice broke into Peter's thoughts.

He shrugged.

"Don't take one," piped up Christine. "Only the little kids take lunch kits."

He nodded and sat down at the table. Once again Christine opened the door below the sink and pulled out a bag, but this time she threw it at Peter. He snatched it from the air and put his lunch in the bag without even looking at what kind of sandwich Mrs. Patterson had made for him.

Although they were supposed to catch the bus, Mrs. Patterson said she would drive them this first day because their backpacks were so heavy. Also, Christine needed to get to school early to practise her "act" for the assembly. Peter sat in the back seat of the van. Andrew and Christine fought for the front seat but Christine won, so Andrew sat in the back beside Peter.

They pulled up in front of Andrew's school first. Andrew jumped out of the van and gave Peter the thumbs-up. "I'll see you after school. Remember our rubber match."

Peter attempted a smile.

"Have a good day, sweetie," said Mrs. Patterson. "Remember to take the bus home."

"Yup. Love you, mom. *Love you, Christine.*"

Christine laughed. "You're such a loser." Then she blew Andrew a kiss.

Peter couldn't keep his mind here in Edmonton. Instead, he thought about how he and Susie horsed around like that, too, but after having the baby, Susie decided to quit school. In fact, lots of kids in Tuk quit school early and didn't go to grade nine. They worked at the gas station or at the bar or one of the restaurants.

Peter wondered if he could find a computer somewhere in the school today. He wanted to e-mail Susie and some of his friends. In Tuk, there was a computer at the school and one at the community centre. He was scared to use the computer at the Patterson house, as it seemed to be Christine's.

After pulling away from Andrew's school, they drove for five minutes before pulling up to a school that was *massive.* Modern and new, it was three times the size of Andrew's school. Kids milled all around the grounds. They stood in groups, talking to one another. Boys chased girls, squirting water from water bottles. Girls dressed like Christine formed clusters. Was anyone alone?

Peter noticed a guy dressed in black who had black hair that stood straight up in spikes standing alone, but then a girl in a black cape approached him. Christine had told him that there were kids who dressed all in black at this school. She called them "the Goth crowd." Peter's stomach flipped at the knowledge that he didn't have a group to belong to. His group was far away, in Tuk. He clutched his backpack tightly.

"Here we are," sang Mrs. Patterson. After she parked the car, she turned back to Peter and smiled. "Are you ready? This is a big step for you. Christine will walk you in and take you to the office. I was going to, but she said that it wouldn't look good. They'll give you a schedule. Then Christine will take you to your homeroom and locker." Mrs. Patterson tapped on the clock in the van. "You're at least fifteen minutes early, so you shouldn't have to rush. Christine says she'll give you a quick tour, too."

Christine jumped out and opened the side door of the van. Smiling, she said, "Come on."

Peter stepped out and wiped his sweaty hands on his jeans. With his head down, he followed Christine up the walk. Was anyone staring at him? Would everyone know he was new?

They went straight to the office. Peter let Christine do the talking. She got his schedule from the front desk, then he followed her down the hall. "You've got Mrs. White for homeroom," Christine said. "She's nice. I had her last year."

Peter nodded.

"Here's your locker. Did you bring the lock?"

Peter pulled it out of his bag.

"Put it on quick so I can show you the rest of the school."

His hands were shaking so much he had a hard time getting the lock to work.

"Here, let me do it," said Christine. "I had trouble with my lock my first year, too."

"It's okay," he mumbled. "I can do it." He forced himself to concentrate.

Just as the lock snapped open, he heard Christine yell, "Hey, Jemma."

"Christine!" Jemma yelled back, running over. She carried

a small portable CD player. "I am so nervous for today."

"Me, too," said Christine.

"Let's find somewhere to practise. I've got the tape."

"Great idea." Christine turned back to Peter, who had his locker open. "Do you think you'll be okay? I know my mom said I'd show you around, but I have to sing today at the assembly. We need to practise."

"I'll be fine," mumbled Peter. All they'd talked about on the way over was Christine singing this morning.

Christine slapped her forehead. "Sorry. Jemma, this is Peter. He's living with us this winter and playing hockey for Sherwood Park."

"Cool," said Jemma. "You in Mrs. White's homeroom?"

Peter nodded.

"Come on, Christine, let's find Madison and Jillian."

Christine pointed down the hall. "The gym is down there, right at the very, very end of the hall. That's where the big assembly will be today. And the library is that way." She pivoted and pointed in the other direction. "The computer lab is right beside the library. What else?" She tapped her hand nervously on her forehead.

"There's Jillian," shrieked Jemma. "Come on, Christine, we've got to go. We're running out of time."

"See ya," said Christine to Peter. "I'll come to your locker after school and take you out to the buses. Make sure you wait for me."

"Okay," said Peter. He turned back to his locker and placed his books on the top shelf. After he hung up his backpack on the hook, he pulled out his schedule. He had English first, then social studies, both subjects with his homeroom teacher. Then they had the assembly. That would be in the gym. He could find his way there. Then lunch. Where was the cafeteria again? Had

Christine told him that? And right after lunch he had science in the lab in room 204. Where was room 204?

He looked down the long hall at all the lockers and at all the kids who were coming into the school. Everyone seemed to know at least one person.

How was he going to find his way around?

7

Welcome

Within five minutes, the halls were totally filled with kids. The noise level escalated. Peter stood in front of his locker, pretending to be busy. He opened and closed his backpack at least three times. He didn't know what else to do. The boy who had the locker beside him didn't talk to Peter, as he was busy talking to another boy.

When the bell rang, everyone around Peter shoved and jostled to get to class. Peter followed a few of the kids into his homeroom. Most ran for the back desks, and two boys collided and sent a desk toppling to the floor. They laughed and pulled it back up. Peter glanced around for an available desk. The only one left was at the front. He didn't want to sit near the front. He didn't recognize anyone from his team.

"Everyone take a seat, please," said Mrs. White.

Peter lowered his head and rushed to the available desk, which was just three seats from the teacher's desk. As soon as he sat down, he took out the notebook that Christine had helped him label *English*. Peter hated English. It was his worst subject for sure. He tapped his fingers on his thighs and jiggled his leg. He couldn't bring himself to look at anyone.

"Welcome to grade eight," said Mrs. White.

The class erupted in cheers. Mrs. White held up her hands.

"I hope everyone had a great summer. I'm looking forward to a terrific year. I want to get started right away with some expectations for the year. But first, I think it's important that I introduce a new student who is attending our school. He's come all the way from Tuktoyaktuk in the western Arctic."

When Peter heard the word Tuktoyaktuk, his body stiffened!

"Peter, why don't you stand up?"

Peter's legs suddenly felt like mushy pudding. His throat was dry. His heart raced. There was no way he could look at anyone. Hair falling in his face, he stared at his desk, placed his hands on it, and pushed himself up.

"Peter will be playing hockey for the Sherwood Park Arrows and has just moved to Edmonton. He's a long way from home, and we want to welcome him to our class."

"Looks like they don't have clothing stores up there." Peter heard the snide whisper through the applause.

He quickly sat back down without glancing up. Why did she have to centre him out?

"Maybe later in the year, when you are feeling a little more at home, you can tell us all about school in the Arctic, Peter." Peter knew Mrs. White was trying to be nice, but he knew even more that he would rather die than do what she was suggesting.

Talk in front of the class? No way.

* * *

Time went by incredibly slowly. Peter kept peering at the clock, but it didn't seem to move at all. Mrs. White talked on and on about what they were going to do over the year in grade eight English. Peter hated reading, and he hated writing even more. How was he to do all the reports she listed on the board? *Novel studies*, *poetry writing*, *limerick writing*. Did everyone already know what a limerick was? They didn't do this much work in Tuk. At least, Peter couldn't remember doing this much.

The social studies agenda wasn't much different. Again, Mrs. White went over what they were going to do for the year. Peter zoned out, and the teacher's words became like one long drone. His thoughts drifted to the hockey practice to come that night — skating, checking, making plays, shooting the puck into the top corner of the net. Reading the ice was so much better, and way easier, than reading a novel. Suddenly, the buzzer went. Peter jumped in his seat and saw everyone hurrying toward the classroom door.

During locker break, Peter put his books away. They had ten minutes before the assembly. Most kids from his homeroom were horsing around in the halls. He wondered where the washroom was. Too embarrassed to ask any of the other students, he went back into the classroom and approached the teacher's desk.

"Mrs. White," he said in a low voice, hoping no one would walk in and hear his question.

"Peter," she smiled. "I am delighted that you are in my class." She raised her eyebrows in a friendly gesture. "What can I help you with?"

"Um, where are the washrooms?"

She stood up and pointed to the door. "Go out the door, turn left, and go down the hall about ten steps. They're on your right-hand side. You can't miss them."

"Thanks," replied Peter.

"How did you find the outline of class expectations this morning?"

He shrugged.

"If you need help, make sure you come see me. I know this is going to be an adjustment for you. I've seen your last year's curriculum and your grades from your old school. I know you haven't covered some of the work most of the students in this class did last year. It's not that you're behind at all, it's just that you worked on some things that were complementary to where you lived. If you ever find yourself stuck, come and see me. It's always better to seek help earlier rather than later." She nodded at Peter. He noticed that when she smiled, her face lit up like a ray of sunshine.

"Okay."

"We've got an assembly after locker break."

He nodded and left the room.

* * *

Peter sat cross-legged onto the floor during the assembly. When Christine and her friends stepped onto the stage for their "act," the entire school clapped. Were they the popular girls? They kind of reminded him of the girls on that *Lizzie McGuire* show on satellite television, the one that Susie loved.

Once they were finished their act, the principal got up to speak. At his school back home, Peter always thought the principal talked way too long, but here, he didn't want her to stop. At least in the gym filled with people he could go totally unnoticed.

But the principal's talk did end.

Next was lunch.

Peter stalled at his locker until the hall was empty. He did not want to go to the cafeteria by himself. It was a beautiful sunny day, so he decided to take his lunch outside. A lot of kids had the same idea. They sat under trees and on the lawn. He started to walk the school grounds, looking around for some-where to hide from everyone else.

Way in the back of the school, he found a secluded spot and

sat on the cement. Even though it took him only five minutes to eat his lunch, he stayed hidden in his little corner until he heard the bell ring, telling him that lunch was over.

* * *

Peter was relieved when the bell finally rang to end the day. At last, time for hockey. He couldn't wait to get on the ice. He shoved his books into his locker, taking only his English book home. It was just the first day, but already he had some home-work to do. It was easy, though. He would be okay to get it done tonight.

Christine had told him she would meet him by his locker and take him to the bus. It wasn't really necessary — he knew where the buses were located and he had his bus number writ-ten down. But what if she came and he was gone?

The halls emptied of students while Peter waited. Where was Christine?

"Peter, are you supposed to be on a bus?" Mrs. White asked as she came out of her classroom.

He nodded. "I'm waiting for someone."

Mrs. White glanced at her watch. "If you're taking the bus home, you'd better go out. They'll be leaving any minute. Do you want me to walk you?"

"No," he said quickly. What would the other kids think if they saw him being walked to the buses by the teacher?

"Do you know your bus number?"

"Yeah."

"Okay, we'll see you tomorrow then."

Peter threw his backpack over his shoulder and headed out the school doors. He heard bus engines revving. The buses were already moving!

He ran toward the long row of yellow school buses. Which one was his? There were so many of them. As he ran, he glanced at the numbers written on the side of each bus, hoping his bus wasn't one of the ones already in motion. He couldn't find bus number eighty-two.

Peter picked up his pace and sprinted. The first bus veered onto the road before Peter got to it. He read the number on the back — eighty-two.

Panting, he stopped.

First day of school and he'd missed the bus. How was he going to get to the Pattersons' place?

Frustrated, he kicked at the stones on the pavement. Why did he wait for Christine? This was all her fault. He should never have listened to her. He was playing by the rules, trying to be a good sport with this new family, but she sure wasn't.

What if this made him late for hockey practice?

8

Late for Practice?

Peter had no idea what to do. He could try to walk home, but he didn't know which way to go, or which streets to take. He hadn't been paying attention that morning when they drove to school.

Maybe he should go back in the school and phone Mrs. Patterson to come pick him up? He had their phone number on a little piece of paper in his backpack. She had said she was working from home today.

His steps slowed as he approached the school doors. He did not want to go back in and ask to use the phone. He felt so stupid. But what other choice did he have? He opened his backpack and took out the paper with the Pattersons' number.

Entering the office, he saw the phone on the front counter. There was a note below the phone: *Please ask before using the phone.*

Peter glanced around. There was no one to ask. He tiptoed toward the phone and quietly picked up the receiver. Staring at his slip of paper, he started to punch the keys when he heard a voice. "Can I help you?"

Startled, he jumped. The phone earpiece fell from his hands, hitting the counter with a thud. A woman with short brown hair stood in a doorway that led down a small hall. "Um," Peter mumbled, his entire body shaking, "I need to use the phone."

"You are supposed to ask first." She unfolded her arms and walked toward Peter. She picked up the dangling earpiece and gently placed it back in the receiver.

"Is your ride not here yet?" she asked.

He shook his head.

"All right, go ahead and make your call. Next time, make sure you ask, okay?"

He nodded. He trembled as he lowered his head, picked up the phone, and punched in the phone number. When he heard Mrs. Patterson's voice on the other end, he said quietly, "It's me, Peter."

"Peter," said Mrs. Patterson, obviously shocked to hear from him. "Shouldn't you be on the bus?"

"I missed it."

"Oh, dear. Didn't Christine meet you after school to take you to the bus?"

Peter twisted the phone cord. "We must have missed each other," he mumbled.

"That's a shame." She paused for a moment and Peter knew she was thinking of a solution. "Let's see. You have practice soon. What I'll do is bring you some food and you can eat in the car. I'll take you right from school to your practice. As soon as Andrew gets home from school, we'll come. I hope we can get you there on time."

"Okay."

"Just wait by the front doors."

When Peter walked back outside, there were still some kids lingering around the front of the school. He purposely avoided them.

Out of the corner of his eye, he could see a boy strolling over to him. "Hey," said the boy, tossing his head back to get his hair out of his eyes, "you're that new kid from the boonies. Do you miss your igloo?"

Peter didn't reply.

"What — don't they teach you to speak where you come from?"

Peter was determined to hold his ground. Even though he was quivering inside, he curled his lip. "Maybe I just don't want to talk to you."

"Leave him alone." A girl came up to the boy and pulled on his shirt.

"You're right. Boonie-boy is not worth my time, that's for sure." The boy flicked Peter's ball cap off his head, laughed, and ran off with the girl, yelling "boonie-boy, boonie-boy!".

Peter bent over and picked up his hat. Then he waited for at least a half-hour before he saw Mrs. Patterson's van. By the time she arrived, he was the only student left on the school grounds.

"Sit in the front, Peter," she said, opening the window.

When he got in, she said, "I'm so sorry this happened to you. I made you a snack. Andrew's bus was late, so he arrived home at the same time as Christine. It's just too bad the rink is closer to home than to the school."

Peter took the plastic container. "Am I going to be late for practice?" he asked.

"Let's hope not."

* * *

Most of the guys were half dressed and the music rocked at full volume when Peter yanked his hockey bag into the dressing room. All eyes were on him. On the drive over, he kept wondering what the guys on this team would say to a player who was

late. At home you could be late — no one cared. But here ...
Coach John had been so firm about no one being late.

He spotted an open seat and immediately sat down. He
pulled out his gear, hoping to get dressed before Coach John
walked through the door.

"You better hurry," said the guy beside him.

Peter strapped on a shin pad. He glanced at the boy. What
was his name again? Tanner?

"Coach John makes you bag skate if you're late."

"What's bag skate?" Peter asked quietly.

"You skate until you puke."

Peter quickly pulled out his socks.

"I'm so pumped to play on Saturday." Tanner said, already
fully dressed. "The team we're playing is good."

Peter wound tape around his leg, then chucked the tape roll
into his bag. He reached for his elbow pads.

"That's what I heard, too," piped up the boy on the other
side of Peter. He spoke in a softer voice. Peter glanced over. The
kid was the same one he sat beside at the first practice.

"I just moved to Edmonton, too," he said to Peter. "So I
don't really know any of these teams. But my dad said Leduc is
good."

"They're good, all right," said Tanner. He chewed on his
mouth guard. "But we have an awesome team. As long as we
play tough, we'll be okay. And we got Stu in net — that's
major."

"You talking about me?" Stu reached over, cranked up the
music even louder, and started to pretend he was rapping.

"You like AC/DC?" asked the boy beside Peter, almost
yelling to be heard.

"It's okay," he replied.

"Are you really from the North?"

"Yeah." Peter did up the Velcro on his shoulder pads.

"I'm from Ontario."

Because Peter had never been to Ontario, he didn't know how to reply.

"What school you at?" the boy continued.

"Sherwood Park Junior High."

"Hey, me too. I hate being the new kid in such a big school. You want to, like, meet up tomorrow? At lunch? I'll look for you. My name's Dylan."

"Sure. Okay." Snatching his practice jersey off the hook, Peter threw it over his head. He was snapping on his cage when Coach John walked in. He breathed a sigh of relief. He had managed to get ready on time. Bag skate? He'd never done that before.

"Hey, guys. Music off."

Stu reached down and shut off the blaster.

"That's better," said Coach John, poking his fingers in his ears. "Now I can hear myself talk. How was your first day of school?"

Everyone booed.

Coach John laughed as he shook his head, then he held up his hand for silence. Peter couldn't believe how fast the room quieted down.

"I noticed a few stragglers. Because it was the first day of school, and you're all dressed and ready now, I'll let it go. But remember my rule — if you're late you either bag skate or don't play the next game. Everyone has the choice." He paused.

Peter looked to the floor.

"Today, we're going to continue our work on puck protection, but we're also going to work on offensive and defensive tactics. I'm going to shuffle you around and try to see who works well in combination. I want to get an idea of the lines I'll play for Saturday night. Defence, I'll make some pair combinations and see how that goes." He held his thumb up. "You work hard and maybe we'll scrimmage at the end of practice, release some of those first day of school kinks."

As soon as he stepped onto the ice, Peter felt his entire body loosen and relax. The sound of his skates crunching on the ice made him stop thinking of the horrible day he'd had at school. He breathed deeply. It felt good to skate.

For the first drill, Peter was paired with Tanner to work on puck protection. Peter had the puck first. Following Coach John's instructions, Peter placed his body between the puck and Tanner, who was applying pressure and trying to take the puck from Peter. Coach John told everyone how important it was to keep the body sealed, to not turn and face. Peter kept his feet moving and held on to the puck. Next it was Tanner's turn to have the puck. Although he tried, Peter couldn't get it from Tanner, either. They worked well, and hard, together, and Peter was sweating by the time Coach John blew the whistle.

With five minutes to go in the practice, Coach John said "We've only a few minutes to scrimmage. Tanner, Glen, and Peter go forward. Peter, you're left wing, Tanner centre, and Glen right."

Peter skated to centre ice while Coach John called out the rest of the lines.

Just before Coach Phil dropped the puck, Tanner skated over to Peter. "I'm going to try and push the puck up, so move as soon as the whistle goes," he said. "You pick it up and skate to centre, and I'll cross over."

Peter nodded. He loved hockey plays. When the puck dropped, he rushed forward. Tanner, who was quick off the draw, smacked the puck. Peter saw the other defenceman moving, but he was already there, thanks to Tanner's plan. Peter picked up the puck and moved to the middle. Tanner swung to the outside. Peter nailed him with a pass, then took off to the net. On his outside drive, Tanner managed to angle toward the net. He wound up for a slapshot. At the side of the net, Peter waited for the deflection. He had to time it just right. As soon as he saw the puck, he put his stick on it, sending it to the top corner.

Tanner rushed over to him.

"Good play!"

"That was an excellent outside drive, Tanner," said Coach Phil. "And Peter, good rush to the net. Let's keep the puck moving, guys. No more face-offs while we scrimmage." Coach Phil sent the puck up the ice.

In the dressing room, Tanner said to Peter, "I like that play we did — the crossover. If we're on a line together, let's try that on Saturday night."

Peter nodded as he unlaced his skate.

Then Dylan, who was sitting on Peter's other side, said, "Where do you want to meet tomorrow? At school. We could eat lunch together."

9

The Deal

When Peter returned to the Pattersons after practice that night, Mrs. Patterson fixed him a snack of cheese and crackers and an apple. At home, Peter always made his own snacks and ate when he wanted to. This was weird. He sure did not feel comfortable going into the fridge to get something, even though Mrs. Patterson said that's what he should do.

"How was school today?" she asked.

"All right," he said, hunching his shoulders to his ears.

"Christine complained that she already has homework."

Shoot. Peter remembered he was supposed to do some English homework tonight. He picked up his plate and took it over to the sink. Susie told him that it was the polite thing to do in someone else's house.

"I'm going to my room."

"Sure," Mrs. Patterson smiled at him. "Do you have homework, too?"

"A little."

"I know Coach John is strict about the school work." She paused, crossed her arms, and nodded her head. "And being late. We have to get you home on time tomorrow. Christine said she went to your locker but you weren't there."

That wasn't true. Peter had left class right away so he

wouldn't miss her. "I, uh, must not have seen her."

Mrs. Patterson picked up her keys. "I know starting a new school is tough. And it's a big school. I'll make sure she meets you tomorrow."

"I can find the bus myself."

"Are you sure?" Mrs. Patterson tilted her head.

"It's not too hard."

"Well, I guess the sooner you figure everything out for yourself, the better it will be for you." She headed to the door that led to the mud room and the garage. "I have to get Andrew from his friend's house."

Peter left the kitchen and went up to his room. He had just sat down at his desk and pulled out his English books when there was a knock on his door.

"Yeah," he mumbled.

The door slowly pushed open. Christine stood leaning on the doorframe.

"I just wanted to say thanks for not telling my mom that I didn't meet you at your locker."

Confused, Peter asked, "Why did you lie?"

Christine stuck her hands in the pockets of her jeans and rolled her eyes. "My mom would kill me if she knew I'd forgotten to meet you. She'd probably ground me."

"I know where the buses are. You don't have to meet me."

"Cool." She bobbed her head. "You got much homework?"

"Not really."

"If you ever need help, let me know. I had Mrs. White last year. I bet I even have some of her old tests kicking around."

"I'll be okay." Peter didn't need help, not if this was all the homework he was going to get every day. This he could handle on his own.

* * *

The next day at school, in every subject, the teachers piled on the homework. By lunch, Peter had so much work to do his head was spinning. He even had a short assignment to do for his tech wheel option class. He didn't understand a lot of the material. He knew he should try to do some of it at school, possibly even get some help from the teacher at lunch, but he was supposed to meet Dylan at the cafeteria. And anyway, how could he tell the teacher he didn't understand already.

As he approached the doors leading to the cafeteria, he slowed down. He hadn't even been in there yet. What if Dylan didn't meet him? What if he couldn't find anyone to sit with? He really didn't want to sit all by himself. He would just have to walk out again and go to his little corner outside. He sucked in a deep breath and headed into the extremely noisy room.

Students sat crowded at tables and it didn't look like there was a single empty seat. Peter noticed the lineup by the food area and the blackboard. Today's special was chili. Peter loved chili, but Mrs. Patterson had made his lunch again. She had said that on Friday, Peter and Christine could both buy, but today was only Wednesday. Peter scanned the big room but didn't see Dylan. Way at the back he saw Tanner and Stu from the hockey team. They were with a bunch of other guys that Peter didn't know. Tanner caught Peter's eye and waved, but then turned to horse around with the guy sitting beside him. Everyone already had their own group. Maybe Dylan had forgotten.

Peter turned to leave. Then he heard his name. When he pivoted, he saw Dylan waving and heading in his direction.

"Peter, I've been waiting for you," said Dylan. He nervously glanced around the big room. "Where do you want to sit?"

Peter saw two people getting up, and he pointed. "How about over there?"

"Sure."

They squeezed through the crowd to plunk down at the table.

"I went to such a small school in Sudbury," said Dylan, pulling out a lunch kit. "This school is huge."

"My school was sort of big, but not like this. We had all grades." Peter pulled out a ham and cheese sandwich from his plastic bag and took a bite. He noticed that some kids carried lunch kits and some didn't.

"Yesterday I ate by myself," said Dylan, picking at his food. "One guy, who thinks he's so cool, threw my lunch kit across the room. After I picked it up, I went right to the library." Dylan munched on a carrot.

"Tomorrow, just bring your lunch in a plastic bag," said Peter. Now he was glad Christine had told him not to bring a kit.

"That's a good idea." Dylan wiped his mouth. "Hey, did you know there are computers in the library so you can go online? I e-mailed a few of my friends back home."

"Really," said Peter. This was great news. He hadn't been able to e-mail anyone yet because he was too scared to use the computer downstairs at the Pattersons' house. Christine was always on it.

"Yeah, you want to go there after we eat?"

"Sure."

They finished eating in less than five minutes. The conversation veered to hockey as they left the cafeteria. "How do you like the team so far?" Dylan asked.

"It's good. I like the practices."

"Yeah. Most of the guys seem okay. I can't wait until Saturday night. My parents both grew up in Edmonton, so they have invited some friends, and my aunt and uncle and cousins are coming, too."

Peter didn't reply. No one was coming to watch him play. His family all lived so far away. He picked up his pace, almost breaking into a run. He couldn't wait to check his e-mail. Before he had left Tuk, he had sat down with Susie and his friends and they had all signed up for e-mail accounts.

In the library, the computers were already logged on to the Internet. The teacher on duty monitored what sites the students were viewing. After waiting five minutes in line, Peter finally sat down in front of a computer screen. He quickly typed in his password. He grinned when he saw he had five new e-mail messages.

"My friends from home sent me mail," he said to Dylan, who was sitting at the computer beside Peter. "And my friend from Calgary."

"You know someone in Calgary?" asked Dylan.

"Yeah, his name is Josh. I met him at summer hockey camp."

"Cool."

Peter opened Susie's mail first.

Hi Pete! Baby Lisa says hi. Not really. She can't talk yet but I think she might have a tooth. Carly and Amy are going to school and like it. The boys don't want to go but Dad says they got to. Dad brought home a caribou last night, so I'm to make soup tonight. Are you doing good? How's your hockey team? I still can't believe you live so far away. We miss you. Have you been to that big mall yet? Susie

Desperately, Peter wished he could see Susie, baby Lisa and all his brothers and sisters. He missed them so much. He decided to open all his e-mails before sending any replies.

Mike and Jason from home told him again how great it was that he was playing hockey on such an amazing team, and how they wished they were as good as he was so they could move away from Tuk and do what he was doing.

Josh asked about his new team. Josh was also playing on a Bantam AAA team. He hoped they would play each other by the end of the year.

Peter was excited to hear from Josh, and thought it would be cool if they did play each other, but the mail from home made him lonesome for his friends and family, for his life in Tuk. He didn't dare tell anyone that life at school here wasn't great — that kids made fun of his clothes, said mean things to him, and threw his friend's lunch kit across the room. And that he lived with a family that included a girl who was a pain.

All his friends thought his life was so great. So Peter wrote to Jason and Mike, telling them how much fun it was to live in Edmonton. He told Susie he would go to the mall soon. He told Josh he loved his team. He had to tell everyone that everything was great, didn't he?

* * *

After school, Peter went straight to the bus. His backpack was bursting with books. How was he going to finish all his homework tonight?

He had just climbed the first step of the bus when Christine came running up and pulled on his shirt. "I'm glad I caught up with you."

Peter didn't reply, but stepped down at her insistent tug.

"I'm not going to catch the bus," she said, panting.

Why was she telling him this? It wasn't like he couldn't ride the bus without her.

"Don't tell my mom, okay? If you keep this between us," she whispered, "I'll help you with your homework."

Why would her parents care, as long as she got home? In Tuk, it didn't matter how you got home, as long as you did. He nodded, then said, "I'd better get on the bus."

Peter boarded the bus, found an empty seat in the middle, and set his backpack on the seat beside him so no one would sit there. Then he stared out the window. The bus ride was long and made Peter's stomach flip-flop. They kept stopping and starting to let kids off, and the bus lurched every time. He'd never ridden a school bus before and he didn't like it much. Finally, Peter recognized his stop. He stood and walked to the front of the bus, ignoring everyone. He knew some of the kids were talking about him — he could hear them snicker. Were they talking about his clothes again?

Once off the bus, he flung his backpack over his shoulder and started to walk toward the Pattersons'. Suddenly, a car drove up beside him and screeched to a stop. The door swung open and Christine hopped out.

"Hey, thanks for the ride, guys." She slammed the car door.

"See you, Chris," said everyone in the car. Then it squealed away from the curb.

Christine winked at Peter. "Remember our deal."

10

English Homework

In the house, Mrs. Patterson reminded Peter that he should help himself to whatever food he wanted. He still didn't feel comfortable going into the Pattersons' fridge, but he was starving. He picked out an apple and a plum from the fruit bowl sitting on the kitchen table. Then he hurriedly went up to his room. Mrs. Patterson asked if he had any problems with the bus. He said no. Fortunately, she didn't ask him anything about Christine.

As he climbed the stairs to his bedroom, he figured he might as well tackle his English homework first. He sat down, placing his books on the desk. He didn't have a desk at home. He usually just worked at the kitchen table.

He went over and over the questions, but he couldn't figure out what to write. He hated writing. After writing a first sentence five times, he crumpled up his paper and tossed it in the garbage. Write a full paragraph! How was he going to finish this? Pushing the other books aside, he decided to read some more of the English book before answering the questions. The teacher wanted the first three chapters of the book, *When Zachary Beaver Came to Town*, read by tomorrow. Peter plumped up his pillow and lay down on the bed to read.

The boy in the book, Zachary Beaver, was the fattest boy in

the world, and people paid money to stare at him. Peter felt sorry for Zachary — he knew what it was like to be stared at because he was different. Zachary just gave in and let people stare at him. Peter thought about how he wanted to give in and try to be a good team player, even when everyone around him made it hard.

Peter was almost finished the second chapter when he heard a knock on his door. "Hey, Peter, you want to play air hockey or mini-sticks downstairs?"

Peter put his book down and went to open his bedroom door.

"Come on, Peter, let's play downstairs," said Andrew, grinning.

Peter smiled, remembering their last go at air hockey. It had been fun. He glanced back at his homework. It wouldn't matter if he left it for a few minutes. "Sure," he said.

They must have lost track of time, because the score in the air-hockey game was 9 – 8 for Peter when Mrs. Patterson called down that it was time for dinner.

"I wish you could play after dinner," said Andrew, "but you have practice. My mom said if it wasn't so late, I could go watch. We'll go to your game on Saturday, though." Andrew glanced at Christine, who was watching television. "Are you coming to the game, Christine?"

She pressed a button on the remote, flipping through the stations. "I might. I'll have to see what my friends are doing. I have volleyball on Saturday."

Then she turned, winked at Peter and asked, "How's that homework?"

"Fine," replied Peter. He didn't want to tell her that the English assignment was hard.

"Remember, if you need help, let me know. I got a ton of homework today. I don't know why they give us so much at the beginning of the year. I mean, why can't we just ease in gradually?"

"I don't have any homework," taunted Andrew.

Peter wished he didn't, either.

* * *

The English homework may have stumped Peter, but the hockey drills sure didn't. He listened carefully to what Coach John said and understood everything.

For the first half of the practice, they worked on hitting and puck protection, and all his aggression toward school came out along the boards. He angled his teammates, then thrust his shoulder into the play. Every hit was clean and powerful.

Halfway through the practice, Coach John blew the whistle. Everyone skated to the white board.

"Next drill is what's called a Continuous Two-on-One." Coach John drew squiggly lines on the white board, demonstrating where the players were supposed to go. "I want to see an aggressive attack and I want you to read the appropriate support off the puck. Defence, make sure of your body position."

Although Peter was eventually paired with everyone, he definitely worked best with Tanner.

In the dressing room after practice, Tanner said to Peter, "We're going to kick some butt this weekend."

"Yeah," Peter grinned. He couldn't wait to play a game!

His good mood lasted until he arrived back at the Pattersons' and saw his books. *Darn*. He didn't get his homework done earlier, and now he was so tired he just wanted to go to bed.

11

Game Against Leduc

The rest of the week flew by. School got harder and harder, and by the end of the week Peter knew he was falling behind. He wondered when Coach John would be checking the marks. He could go in for help at lunch, but then he wouldn't have time to go to the library and check his e-mail. Getting e-mail from home was the highlight of his time at school, but after every lunch he felt very lonely for all his friends and family.

Christine didn't catch the bus once all week, but after the first day Mrs. Patterson didn't ask Peter again about the bus. He figured there was no need to say anything.

Finally Saturday arrived, the day of his first game. Even though it was only an exhibition match, Peter woke up excited. He lay in bed, thinking of the plays he would make — how he would pass and shoot and move to the net for the rebounds. As he sat up, he saw his books piled on his desk. He moaned and flopped back down on his bed. He hated school.

After breakfast, Peter was going to crack open his books and take a stab at his work, but Andrew begged him to play mini-sticks. They set up the nets and decided on teams. Andrew called dibs on the Edmonton Oilers, so Peter went for the Nashville Predators. Jordin Tootoo, an Inuk from Nunavut, played for that team.

Andrew made the rules and actually put a twenty-minute

timer on so they would know when the period was over. Between periods, they went upstairs for water and cookies. During the third period, Andrew had to go to the washroom. Peter stayed downstairs to shoot the plastic puck. He had just flung one into the top corner of the net when Christine walked out of her bedroom.

"My friends and I are coming to your game tonight," she said.

Peter nodded and tapped the plastic hockey stick against his hand, not sure what to say.

"It should be a good game," she continued. One of my friends sort of likes one of the guys on your team."

Why was she telling him this? Peter couldn't care less.

"Boy, you don't say much, do you? Don't you, like, want to know which guy?"

"Not really," he said, bending the stick slightly.

"Okay, play it your way." She paused, then asked, "Hey, how's your homework going?"

"Uh, I don't know."

"How can you not know?" She tossed her head, flinging her hair. After putting it in a ponytail, she said, "I meant what I said, you know. I don't mind helping you if you need help. When I make a deal, I make a deal."

"Well, okay," said Peter rather quickly. He wasn't sure why he agreed — it was as if the words just popped out of his mouth.

"Are you saying you want help?"

"Yeah, I guess."

"Why don't you go get your books and meet me in the kitchen after you finish your game with Andrew? I'm not going out till later."

Peter had to accept Christine's offer. How long would it take before Coach John realized Peter wasn't doing so well in school?

By the end of just one hour of working with Christine, Peter couldn't believe how much they'd accomplished. Christine went over what Mrs. White looked for in English assignments and even took the time to rewrite one of Peter's chapter responses so he could get the hang of how to do it. She said she'd help on every one if he liked. She also gave him all her old social studies notes and a project she'd done on Brazil. She helped him with his math problems. Maybe she was okay after all.

* * *

Peter walked into the dressing room for the exhibition game that night feeling confident and ready to play.

Stepping onto the ice, he glanced at the big crowd that had come to watch the game. He wished his dad could be in the stands. At home in Tuk, there wasn't a lot of entertainment, so a hockey game drew a big crowd. The few bleachers in the arena were always filled for hockey games, and a lot of people stood along the boards, too. He missed his friends chanting his name and his little brothers climbing over the glass to wish him luck. He had been their hero, the big star. Now he was just one of many.

Peter was put on left wing, on a line with Tanner and Greg. He worked well with Tanner, but Greg was a bit of a puck hog. Didn't matter, though, they all had to play hard.

When he heard his line would be out first, Peter got really pumped. After the team cheer, he swigged some water and skated to his position. Peter glanced around. The ref, dressed in the official uniform, stood at centre ice. There were even linesmen. Peter had never played in a big game like this before. At home, friends would ref. He had knots in his stomach and his hands were sweating.

The whistle blew. The puck dropped.

Tanner fought hard to gain possession. He slapped it back to Dylan, who was on defence. Peter flew up his wing. Dylan sent it to him, but the pass was too long. Peter reached his stick out but couldn't get it on the end. The defence for the Leduc team raced forward and picked up the puck. Was the defence going to pass or make a rush? Peter read a rush. Seeing the player along the boards, Peter headed toward him. Shoulder first, he bashed into the player to knock him off the puck. When he made the hit, he heard the boards quake.

Leduc lost possession. The puck was loose. Peter darted to the puck and picked it up. Then he looked up. Tanner was behind the net and Greg was over by the boards on the other side. Both of his defencemen were in position along the blue line. Because Tanner wasn't yet tied up, Peter nailed him with a hard pass.

The Leduc defence swooped in on Tanner, but he quickly passed to Greg on the boards. *Send it to the back,* thought Peter. Greg was at a bad angle to the net, but he made the shot anyway. The goalie made a stick save and batted the puck over to the boards.

Peter flew toward it, managing to get the puck on the end of his stick. What should he do? He quickly looked around. Tanner was now tied up behind the net. Greg was out of position.

Peter swatted the puck back to Dylan and rushed to the side of the net. Dylan wound up for a slapshot. Peter watched the puck move through the air, and when it was close, he tried for a deflection. The puck pinged off the top crossbar and onto the glass. The whistle blew.

Peter skated to the bench. Coach John tapped his helmet. "Great shift, Peter. Keep cycling the puck. Your hits along the boards are working, too. They're clean and hard — keep them that way."

At the end of the first period, there was no score. Peter couldn't believe it when the doors at the end of the rink lifted for the Zamboni to come out. Did they clean the ice after every period?

Coach John held up his white board in the dressing room. "Wingers," he said, "I want you to get the puck deep in their zone. Centres, I want you to play quarterback. Get the puck and look for the play. Use your point men. If you can't get a decent shot on net, send it back. Then rush in for the deflection. Peter has been the only player to make that play so far."

When Peter heard his name, his face grew hot under his helmet. He stared straight ahead, knowing some of the guys had glanced his way.

Back on the ice, Peter's line was put out first again. Tanner tapped Peter with his stick and said, "Off the faceoff, I'm going to get it back to the defence."

"Okay," Peter nodded. "I'll go up my wing."

"I'll tell Greg to cut to the middle for the pass." Tanner skated over to Greg while Peter lined up on his wing.

This time they had to score. Someone had to get on the scoreboard, and it might as well be them. Peter got in his crouch, ready to move. The ref went to drop the puck, but Tanner moved too quickly. The ref straightened up and Tanner skated away from the faceoff circle toward Peter. The ref motioned for Peter to skate to centre. This had never happened to Peter in a game before, but he'd seen it all the time in NHL games on TV.

He bent over, squared his shoulders to the ice, curled his bottom hand over his stick, and stared at the ice, waiting for the puck to drop. Timing was everything — the puck would be in view only for a split second. When he saw the black flash, he made his move. Hitting it, he sent it back to Dylan on defence. Dylan picked it up. As Tanner moved to his centre position, Peter skated to his wing. Dylan sent to the puck to Greg on right wing.

In practice, they had done a three-on-two drill in which Peter swung to the middle. Peter hit the blue line before Greg and dragged his foot so he wouldn't go offside. As soon as Greg was over the line, Peter sped to the net. Instead of passing, Greg made a wrist shot. Peter scrambled for the rebound, but was hit from behind by a Leduc player and landed on top of the goalie. Tanner dashed out front and chipped the puck into the top corner.

The ref blew the whistle and waved his arms. No goal. Goalie interference.

"What?" chirped Tanner. "What about the hitting from behind?"

The Leduc defenceman pushed his face against Tanner's. Tanner pushed him. Seeing an altercation starting, Peter quickly skated over to Tanner and grabbed him by the back of his shirt. "Don't get into it. He's not worth it. Let's get it back. We can score here."

Tanner shrugged Peter off and straightened his jersey. Then he skated to the faceoff circle. Greg lined up behind Peter for the faceoff, which was in Leduc's end. The Leduc goalie squatted low and stared straight ahead.

Tanner won the faceoff and sent it back to Dylan, who stickhandled a few times, then sent it across the ice to his defence partner. Peter moved to the boards to give him someone to pass to. Once he had the puck on his stick, Peter searched for his open man. Tanner, behind the net, started to move out front. This was it!

Peter made a hard pass to the side of the net. When the puck landed on Tanner's stick, he flipped it up and over the goalie's shoulder. It was in! He jumped in the air and raced to Peter, giving him a high-five.

"Great pass," exclaimed Tanner.

"You were right there," said Peter.

"Awesome goal, you guys," said Dylan, skating up to the group.

"Come on, we can do it again next shift," said Tanner.

The score at the end of the game was 1–0 for Sherwood Park. Peter had never played in such an intense game in his whole life. Even at elite hockey camp, the final game hadn't been like this. They hadn't been a *real* team.

Now, this was hockey!

12

Waiting for Christine

That night, after returning to the Pattersons', Peter phoned home to talk to his family. He had to tell them about the game. As excited as he was, when he hung up the phone he felt a funny twinge in his stomach. He wished they could have seen him play today, wearing his new team helmet and gloves, just like ones the pros wear.

"I'm going to my room," said Peter to Mr. Patterson.

"That was a good game today, Peter." He put his hand on Peter's shoulder. "You play a tough, clean game of hockey. I'm impressed. You keep at it and you're in for a solid year."

Peter nodded. He never knew what to say to Mr. Patterson.

"I mean it," said Mr. Patterson. "Maybe one weekend when you don't have a game we can drive to one of Trevor's games. It would be good for you see that kind of hockey, too."

"Really?" Peter would love to see a Major Junior game. One day he wanted to play on a Major Junior team. He just wished he didn't have to live so far away from home to do it.

* * *

The next few weeks flew by. Peter managed to do okay with his school work, mainly because Christine continued to help him.

She never once caught the bus and instead always got a ride home with her high-school friends. Peter met her when he got off the bus, since she insisted that they walk home together. She said he had to wait for her, or she wouldn't help him with his homework.

Every day for lunch, Peter met up with Dylan, then they went to the library together to check their e-mails. But the e-mails Peter was getting from his friends were dwindling. The first week they replied right away, but then they started to slack off. Even Susie. This made Peter feel sad. Hearing about home was the highlight of his day. Well, that and hockey practice.

Coach John had wanted to get some good solid practices in, so he hadn't scheduled any more exhibition games. But the time had finally come — they were playing Fort McMurray on the weekend in their big season opener!

* * *

On the Thursday before the Saturday game, Peter jumped off the bus, knowing he had to hurry. His team had an early after-school practice, the last one before the weekend game. Mr. Patterson said he would drive Peter to his practice because Mrs. Patterson had some sort of meeting.

As Peter waited for Christine, he thought about the major English project that was due the next day. He still had a lot to do before he handed it in. He hoped Christine would help him after his practice — if she didn't, there was no way Peter could get it finished. After waiting five minutes for Christine at the bus stop, Peter started to get anxious. Where was she? He had to get his equipment organized and eat something before practice.

Five more minutes passed and Peter knew he had to get home. If he was late for practice he'd have to bag skate or miss the big game. So far, only Greg had had to bag skate. Peter did not want to be the next.

He tapped his foot and twisted his back to shuffle his backpack, which was heavy with books. Every night he had to take home so much homework. Again, he thought about the dumb English assignment he had to do. He still had to write five chapter responses.

Where was Christine? If she didn't hurry, he was going to be late. This was so unfair of her. Peter felt the anger and impatience growing inside him, ready to erupt. He had never felt this way at home, like he was being forced into a situation he had no control over.

Finally, Peter got tired of waiting and didn't care any more about Christine and being a good sport for her. If she got in trouble, then she got in trouble. He started walking toward the house. He had just turned his back when he heard a car come squealing around the corner. It braked and screamed to a stop. Peter turned around to see Christine sitting in the front, laughing.

"Hey, Peter," she said, grinning and hanging out the window. "Don't go without me."

The boy driving pulled at her belt and she toppled back into the car, still laughing. Peter fumed. He didn't want to wait for her.

"I've got practice," he said angrily.

"I'm coming, I'm coming." This time she burst into giggles. Then she turned to the boy and kissed him. Peter groaned and turned so he wouldn't see them. After a few minutes, when Christine was still not out of the car, he clenched his fists at his side. *They were still kissing. Gross.*

Peter had to go! Head down, he started marching down the sidewalk. He heard the car door slam. Then Christine yelled, "Wait for me!"

Peter kept walking and let her catch up to him.

"How was school?" she asked breathlessly.

"Fine," Peter replied.

"Do you have much homework?"

He didn't answer.

"Why are you walking so fast?"

"I'm going to be late."

"Oh, so-o-rry."

When they entered the house, Mr. Patterson was standing in the kitchen with his coat on and car keys in hand. "Where were you two? I was just heading out to find you."

Christine rolled her eyes. "The bus had a breakdown."

Shocked, Peter just stared at her. How could she lie like that?

Mr. Patterson looked at his watch. "Peter, I have to get you to the rink. Grab your gear."

Peter took the stairs two at a time to get to his room. He threw his books on his bed and quickly snatched what he needed for practice. When he got to the bottom of the stairs, Christine was waiting for him. "Don't tell my dad about Brad," she mouthed.

"And what if I do?" he snapped back.

* * *

On the drive over, Mr. Patterson hit every red light. Peter had never seen such heavy traffic. In Tuk, no matter what, you could never be late for practice. You could always go straight to the rink. Right now, Peter just wished he was snowmobiling to the rink, instead of sitting in Mr. Patterson's idling car.

"Must be an accident," said Mr. Patterson, craning his neck to see past the side of the transport truck in front of them.

Peter clutched the door handle and didn't reply.

"Where did the bus break down?" asked Mr. Patterson.

"Um." What was he supposed to say? *The bus didn't break down.* "I'm not sure," he said with a shrug.

"It's too bad it broke down on the night of your early practice. Do you want me to tell your coach for you?" He glanced at the clock on the dashboard. "There's no way I'll get you there on time now."

"No, that's okay," said Peter quickly, staring out the window. He couldn't have Mr. Patterson lie. What if Coach John found out that the bus didn't break down? Then how would Peter explain? Peter was so mad at Christine. And he was tired of playing by her rules.

"You sure?"

Peter nodded.

Mr. Patterson dropped Peter off in front of the arena. Peter raced to the dressing room. When he flung the door open, Coach John was already talking to the rest of the team, using the white board to explain the drills. Peter's face prickled with heat. He saw Dylan glance at him and slide over to make space. Peter lowered his head and tugged his bag to the empty spot.

Coach John paused for just a moment to stare at Peter before he started talking again. Peter was halfway through dressing when Coach John put the white board down.

"One more thing, guys. Listen up, now."

The room quieted to a hush. "I'm going to be checking your marks before our game on the weekend. I'm calling each of your teachers tomorrow to find out how you're doing. If anyone is not pulling their weight at school, they won't play in Saturday's game."

Peter was still tying his skates when Coach Phil poked his head in the door and said, "Ice is ready."

The guys filed out, leaving just Peter and Coach John in the room. "Anything you'd like to say, Peter?"

Should he lie? Say the bus stalled. No, he couldn't do that. He could say they were in traffic. Was that a good excuse? When he tried to speak, his entire mouth dried up and he could not get one word out.

"Well, at least you're not into excuses. You know I have to skate you for the first part of the practice."

Peter kept his head down and nodded.

"I won't be too hard on you, okay? But rules are rules. I can't exempt one person, or the rule has no meaning."

Again, Peter's mouth felt as if it was filled with dry dust, so he just nodded.

"When you get on the ice, I want you to see Coach Phil."

As Peter stepped onto the ice, he saw the guys huddled around Coach John over at the white board. Then he saw Coach Phil. With a sick feeling in his stomach, he skated toward him.

13

English Assignment

Peter skated and skated — back and forth across the width of the ice. He could hardly catch his breath before he heard Coach Phil blow the whistle for another set. The muscles in his legs burned. When Coach Phil said he was finished, Peter bent over at the waist to catch his breath.

Everyone stared at Peter as he skated to the bench, but no one said anything. Peter gulped down some water, wishing everyone would stop looking at him.

For the rest of the practice, Peter was determined to work hard to make up for being late. He pushed and pushed. At the end of the practice he had cramps in his legs.

In the dressing room, he plunked down beside Dylan, leaned back, and closed his eyes. He had never been this tired.

"Boy, were you flying out there," said Dylan. "I thought you'd be done in after all that extra skating." Dylan downed the remains of the water in his bottle. Then he leaned in toward Peter. "Was it hard? The skating?" he whispered.

"It was okay." Peter slugged back water as well.

Greg sat on the other side of Peter. "I threw up when I had to skate," he said. "You probably got off easy because we have a game on Saturday and Coach John doesn't want his *star* player to be tired."

Of all the guys on the team, Greg was the only one who liked to take jabs at Peter. Peter didn't think of himself as the star player. Not on this team. This whole mess was about being late, and it was all Christine's fault. No more lying for her. Peter had had it.

"Hey, Peter," said Dylan quietly.

Peter turned to look at Dylan.

"You want to go to the West Edmonton Mall on Saturday? We could hang out a bit before the game. We probably shouldn't go to the water slides, but we could go to the arcade. My mom said she could pick you up. I can get her to call the family you're staying with."

"Sure," said Peter. At least he'd have something to write to Susie about, instead of telling her how he was late for practice and had to skate hard for fifteen minutes.

* * *

Mr. Patterson met Peter in the arena lobby.

"How was practice, Peter?" he asked as they walked out to the car.

"Okay."

"You've got a big game on Saturday night."

Peter nodded.

On the drive home, Mr. Patterson asked, "Do you have much homework to do?"

"I have some English," Peter said quietly.

"I don't think Christine has anything on tonight. Maybe she can help you."

Peter didn't reply. He didn't want to take help from *her*.

As soon as Peter entered the kitchen, he saw Christine leaning against the counter, sipping on a juice box. "Hi, Peter," she said casually.

Peter glared at her and didn't reply.

She smiled sweetly at him until her father had walked out of the room. Then she whispered, "You didn't say anything to him, did you?"

"No, but I should have," he replied angrily.

"Whew." She dramatically heaved a sigh of relief. "I'll make this up to you, I promise."

"Don't bother."

Peter headed up to his bedroom. There, he yanked his novel and notebook out of his backpack. He groaned. How was he going to write five chapter responses in one night?

He leaned back in his chair and threw his pencil on the desk. What was the use?

What if he just didn't hand it in? Would Coach John find out tomorrow when he called his teacher? Would he not let him play on Saturday?

A knock shook his door.

"Who is it?"

"It's me, Christine."

What did she want? He stood, opened the door, and let her in.

"My dad says you have homework and that I should see if you need help."

"Well, I don't."

"Are you sure?"

"Why did you lie to your dad?" he asked. "The bus didn't break down."

She shoved her hands into her jeans pockets. "My parents hate Brad. They have forbidden me to go out with him."

"Why?"

"They say he's too old for me and that he drives his car too fast. I'm not supposed to get rides from him."

"But you do every day."

"Yeah, and don't you tell or I won't help you with your homework anymore." She crossed her arms and raised her eyebrows. "And you need help. I know Coach John will kick you off the team if you don't get good grades."

"Look, I don't need or want your help again." Peter shook his head. He stared down at his work until he heard Christine leave his room.

* * *

The next day at school, Peter handed in his project even though it was only half finished. At least he'd handed in something. He figured the teacher wouldn't read it that day, and maybe he would be able to play on the weekend.

After school, Peter was surprised when Christine met him at the bus. "Peter," she said, "if my mom asks you anything about where I am, tell her I went to Jemma's after school." She winked. "I'll help you with your homework." She almost sang when she talked. "I heard the grade eights have a *huge* science test next week."

"Why don't you phone your mother and tell her yourself?"

"I did. But just in case she asks, you tell her you saw me with Jemma, see?" Christine waved to someone and Peter turned around to see Jemma waving back. "I've got to go. Remember, do what I say and I'll help you study for science and stay on the hockey team."

Peter boarded the bus. Christine was so annoying.

As soon as he walked through the door at the Pattersons', Andrew came running up to him. "Where's Christine?"

"At her friend's."

"Which friend?"

"Jemma, I think."

"Mom," Andrew yelled. "Christine did go to Jemma's."

Mrs. Patterson walked into the kitchen. "Did you see her leave, Peter?"

"Yeah," he nodded. He hadn't really seen her leave, but what did that matter?

"Has Christine been ..." Mrs. Patterson clasped her hands together. "Has she been catching the bus lately?" She looked at him, forehead furrowed, waiting for his answer.

Peter cringed inside. What was he supposed to say? Peter didn't want to answer Mrs. Patterson. Why did she always have to ask him questions about Christine? It wasn't like it was his job to babysit or spy on her.

"Um." He shrugged and sort of nodded his head. He found he couldn't tell on Christine, not unless he wanted to be a big snitch.

"So, she *has* been on the bus. Well, that's good." Mrs. Patterson turned, picked up a dishrag, and wiped the counter.

Andrew said, "Come on, Peter, let's play mini-sticks. And I have a game later. Will you come watch me?"

"Sure," said Peter. Any excuse would do to get out of the kitchen and away from Mrs. Patterson and her questions. All this family thought about was Christine and what she was and wasn't doing, and they made it hard to play as a team. Christine was like Greg, the puck hog. Peter was seething inside.

"Maybe we'll all go," said Mrs. Patterson. Her friendly smile made Peter feel even worse for being so angry.

"Oh, by the way, Peter," she said. "I had a phone call from Dylan's mother. I guess you two are headed to the West Edmonton Mall tomorrow. You'll have to take it easy before the big game. No water slides."

"You're lucky," said Andrew. "You have to go on the rides in Galaxy Land."

"I'll take you boys one day when Peter doesn't have a game, so you can go in the pool."

Andrew turned to Peter, his eyes as big as pucks. "You just *have* to go on the big slide. It is *so* fun." Andrew bobbed up and down.

Peter tried to smile at Mrs. Patterson and act excited, but he felt horrible.

14

West Edmonton Mall

Peter awoke the next morning and went downstairs, but no one was up. He helped himself to cereal and milk. The night before, Christine had come home late and brought Jemma to sleep over. At least with Jemma there, Peter didn't have to talk to Christine.

He looked at the clock on the kitchen oven. It was only eight, and Dylan wasn't picking him up until ten. He knew he should go upstairs and try to tackle some of his homework, so he trudged back up to his room.

He took one look at his books and moaned. He hated all this school work. Why did he have to do all this dumb work to be a hockey player? Why was Coach John so strict about school? In the North, school was important but not this important. Lots of kids never went to high school. They were too busy hunting and fishing.

He opened up his science book. There was so much material, he didn't know where to start. As he tried to study, his mind wandered. He wondered what all his friends were doing. Already it was nearing October, so the weather would be changing. Snow usually fell in November. The ice road would be opening in another couple of months, too. Hockey didn't start in the Arctic until it got cold, as the arena used real ice. In

Mike's last e-mail, he had said that they had made the drum dancing teams already. Peter would have been on Mike's team if he were home.

Peter put his book down and went to his closet. He hadn't taken his drum from its hiding place since he arrived. He pulled it out. A layer of dust sat on the top of it. Peter blew it off and sat down on his bed. As everyone was still sleeping, he knew he would have to be quiet. He softly tapped his fingers on the taut caribou hide that covered the drum, the rhythm coming naturally. He closed his eyes, leaned back against the wall, and started to softly throat sing. Suddenly, his body relaxed and he forgot about everything — all the homework he had to do, Christine and her lies, being late for practice.

He continued singing, the vibrations in his throat making familiar loon-like sounds, and he beat his drum with his fingers. Suddenly, he opened his eyes to see his door was slightly open.

He quickly put the drum down and went to the door. There were Christine and Jemma, sitting on the floor outside his room.

"What are you doing?" Peter asked.

"Listening to you." Christine stood. She wore a big smile. "That was awesome, Peter. Can we see your drum?"

"Yeah, I guess." He didn't think he could have sounded that good, as he was trying so hard to be quiet.

"You should enter the talent show at the school," said Jemma. She touched the drum gently. "You'd, like, win for sure."

"No way," said Peter. Playing in front of the whole school? That was the last thing Peter wanted to do.

Both Jemma and Christine wanted to try the drum. He showed them a few rhythms and they all laughed when Christine tried to throat sing.

They were all still playing around when Mrs. Patterson called upstairs. "Peter, Dylan will be here soon."

"Hey, Peter, we'll meet you downstairs, okay?" Jemma and Christine skipped out of Peter's room. At the doorframe, Christine turned and said, "Thanks for the singing and drum lessons. That was cool."

"Are you excited to go to the mall?" asked Mrs. Patterson when Peter walked into the kitchen.

"Yeah."

"There's a big ice rink right in the middle of the mall," said Christine. The two girls were munching on cereal.

An ice rink? In a mall? Peter had never been to a mall before. "Do all malls have ice rinks?"

Christine laughed. "No, just West Ed." Then she sighed. "Wish I was going to the mall today. Jemma and I have volleyball practice and then we're going to the library." She winked at Jemma just as the doorbell rang.

"That must be Dylan and his mother," said Mrs. Patterson, wiping her hands on a towel.

Peter followed her to the front door. Since he was all ready to go, Dylan's mother and Mrs. Patterson spent only a few minutes talking before they got to leave.

Just as Peter was about to walk out the door, Mrs. Patterson handed him a twenty-dollar bill. "Buy yourself something," she said.

"Thanks," he whispered.

* * *

Peter read the signs for the West Edmonton Mall from the car window. The closer they got, the more he fidgeted. He thought of Susie and wished she was here with him, although he knew he might have to coax her through the front doors. Susie thought Yellowknife was big and scary. What would she think of this?

Dylan's mother dropped them off at the main entrance to the mall. She would pick them up in time to get home and rest before the big game.

Totally shocked at the size of the mall, Peter remained speechless as they entered. He looked up and down, staring at everything. He could hardly believe it — there was a replica of a big ship and water, and even an underwater area. Surrounding the big ship were stores and more stores, and there was a bridge over the water for people to walk on. And everywhere he looked were people. Dylan and Peter stood by a railing on the second floor. Peter tilted his head to glance way up at the big roof made completely of windows. Then he looked down at the ship and the water. He even thought he saw a submarine floating underwater. This mall was almost as big as all of Tuk!

When he turned from the railing, he saw the waterpark. He pulled on Dylan's shirt and they ran to the window to look inside. Waves rolled in and out in a pool area and … the slides were tunnels! People ran into the water and splashed down the slides. Peter had never been to a waterpark.

"That slide is the best." Dylan pointed to the tallest slide, which looked as if it went straight down. Peter had to look way up to see to the top of the slide.

"I don't know," said Peter, squinting. "Have you been down it before?" It looked awfully long.

Dylan nodded. "Yup. It's so steep, sometimes you get a wedgie."

Peter giggled. Then he pointed at a smaller slide. "I'd start with that one."

"Maybe we can do the waterpark next time. Let's walk around a bit. My mom is picking us up at three, so we have lots of time. We can go to Galaxy Land."

"Is there really an ice rink in here, too?"

"Yeah, let's go see that first."

Peter gawked at everything as they made their way through the crowds to get to the rink. All he could think of was e-mailing Susie to tell her he'd gone to the mall and it was even bigger than he had imagined. When they got to the rink, there was a huge crowd gathered.

"Wonder what's going on," said Dylan. "The two times I've been here with my family, there's just been figure skaters. Sometimes they have public skating, too. We should come one day with our skates."

Peter didn't answer because he was too busy reading a sign. "Dylan! *The Oilers are practising here today!*"

"That's why there's such a crowd," exclaimed Dylan. "Come on, let's get closer."

Peter and Dylan nudged through the crowds to get right to the front. Peter's mouth dropped open as he watched Ryan Smyth skate by him in a two-on-one drill. He was so close that Peter could see the sweat on his face.

"They're doing that drill we did in practice the other day," whispered Dylan.

Peter watched Ryan Smyth fire the puck. His shot was like a rocket.

"I wonder if we can get autographs when they get off," said Dylan, his eyes lighting up. "Let's go find some scrap paper and wait by the gate. I've got a pen."

Obviously other kids had the same idea as Peter and Dylan. There was a huge mob by the gate, and they had to get into line. After fifteen minutes of waiting, Peter saw the players coming toward the crowd of kids.

Dylan moved in closer and pulled Peter with him. "Come on, Pete," he whispered. "This is our chance."

Worried he'd get lost in such a big crowd, Peter followed

Dylan closely. When Dylan thrust out his pen and paper, so did Peter. Ryan Smyth signed Dylan's first, then he took Peter's paper. "Do you have a pen?" he asked Peter, looking him straight in the eye.

Peter just stared. He didn't know what to say. Dylan thrust the pen at the NHL player. "Here, use mine."

Ryan signed his name and smiled when he handed Peter the paper. Peter felt as if he was stuck to one spot. He watched as Ryan signed more autographs, then skated to the other side of the rink toward a lady holding a baby. He shook off his glove and reached over to touch the baby's hair. The baby looked to be about a year older than baby Lisa.

"That must be his kid," said Dylan.

"I can't believe I got his autograph!" exclaimed Peter. "Wait till the guys at home hear this."

"Come on." Dylan tugged on Peter's shirt. "Let's go to Galaxy Land."

The time sped by. Galaxy Land was fun, but Peter refused to go on the big roller coaster. It looked way too fast. Dylan loved all the fast rides. They did the Drop of Doom and Peter felt like his stomach was in his mouth when they landed. Peter loved the arcade area, where they played basketball for at least an hour.

All too soon, it was time to meet Dylan's mom. They both wanted to hit the candy store first, which was located right outside the waterpark. Both boys were going to save the candy for after the game.

Inside the store were bins upon bins of candy. Peter was scooping out some red cherry jelly beans when he heard a giggle. He looked up, to see Christine over by a basket full of suckers. She was with Jemma and … two guys! Peter watched as the guy he now knew was Brad put his arm around her. Wasn't she supposed to be at volleyball and the library?

Peter didn't want Christine to see him. How was he to get out of this store? He clutched his two bags of candy — he wanted to get some for Andrew — and moved to the counter.

Suddenly, Dylan yelled from the other side of the store. "Hey, Peter, get a load of these."

Peter cringed. When he glanced up, Christine was staring at him. "Hi, Peter," she said sweetly. Too sweetly.

"Uh, hi." He handed the salesclerk his money.

Christine sauntered over to him and whispered, "You never saw me here, right?"

Peter didn't answer.

"You can't tell my parents."

"Okay, okay." He picked up his candy and left the store with Dylan right on his heels.

15

Another Lie

It was three-thirty when Dylan's mom dropped Peter off at the Pattersons'. He hopped out of the car and ran toward the house. Today had been fun. Maybe living in Edmonton wasn't so bad. But once he hit the porch landing, he slowed down. This was the first time he had to walk in the house alone. Should he knock?

No, he lived here now.

He pushed open the door, excited to give Andrew the candy he'd bought for him. When he entered the house, no one greeted him. He could hear someone talking in the kitchen. He walked down the hall toward the worried voices.

"Why didn't she go to her volleyball practice? Where could she be?" Mrs. Patterson sounded as if she was crying. Peter stopped.

Mr. Patterson said, "She's probably at someone's house."

"I've tried everyone. No one has seen them."

"What about that girl she hung out with last year? Allison?"

"I tried her, too."

"What about her teammates? Could she have gone with them?"

"When her coach called, I couldn't believe they weren't at practice. You dropped them off."

"Could she be with that Brad fellow?"

"She promised me she wouldn't see him again. I believe her. I just hope nothing has happened to them. I wish the police would do something now! Instead of ... instead of waiting for twenty-four hours to file a missing persons report. I just can't wait that long." Mrs. Patterson was sobbing.

The police! But Christine was at the mall. With Brad. Peter had to tell them.

Hand on his forehead, Mr. Patterson came into the hallway. "Peter. I didn't hear you come in," he said in a low voice as he rubbed his chin. "Did you have a good time at the mall?" He opened the closet door and took out his coat.

Peter nodded. "Uh, Mr. —"

"I'm going for a drive. I'll be back shortly."

Peter went into the kitchen. Andrew sat at the kitchen table. His face was white as snow. Peter handed him the candy, his hand shaking. Mrs. Patterson was busy talking on the phone and had her back turned to Peter.

"Thanks," said Andrew to Peter.

"Christine's missing," Andrew whispered. "They think she might have been kidnapped."

Kidnapped! Peter had to tell Mrs. Patterson that Christine was at the mall. How long would she be on the phone?

"They left around ten this morning." Mrs. Patterson paused, wiping her eyes with a tissue. When she saw Peter, she sadly waved. "I've tried everyone." She wiped her nose.

Peter waited patiently. When she finally hung up, he said, "Um, Mrs. Patterson."

"I just can't believe this." Mrs. Patterson obviously didn't hear him.

Peter tried again. "*Um.*"

Mr. Patterson walked through the kitchen door, coming in

from the garage. "I forgot my phone."

"Hey …" Peter tried once more.

Suddenly there was a sound at the front door. Everyone looked at each other, then Mr. and Mrs. Patterson raced out of the kitchen and into the hallway. Peter and Andrew followed.

"Christine!"

"Hi." For once she didn't bounce when she spoke.

"Where have you been?"

Peter stepped into the hallway. Christine shot him a glance. He could tell by the look on her face she knew that her parents were extremely upset and that she was in trouble. She looked back at her parents and said, "Didn't Peter tell you?"

Everyone stared at Peter. "Tell us what?"

"I saw him at the mall and told him to tell you Jemma and I met up with Sandy and that we were going to a movie. She's real nice. Her mom said she'd give us a ride home."

16

Against the Boards

Mrs. Patterson snapped her head around to stare at Peter. "Why didn't you say something when you walked through the door? You must have seen how worried we were."

Peter's mouth gaped. "I, uh, tried." He couldn't finish — he had no idea what to say. Peter stared at Christine. How could she have involved him in this? She avoided eye contact and stared at the floor.

"Christine," said Mr. Patterson. "Why didn't you go to volley-ball practice? Your coach phoned, you know."

"Jemma and I thought it was cancelled, Dad," she said. "No one was there when we got there, and then Sandy showed up five minutes later."

"What do you mean, no one was there?"

"We waited for fifteen minutes and no one showed up, so we decided to leave. I guess we got our times mixed up. I left a message, telling you I was going to the mall instead. Then when I saw Peter I told him to tell you, too."

"We didn't get a message."

"Really. I left one. Maybe something happened with the phone company. Jemma said she left one for me the other day that I didn't get. That is so weird."

Peter couldn't believe his ears. Christine had a comeback

lie for everything.

"Who is this Sandy?" Mr. Patterson asked.

"She's new to the team. I'm sorry I caused you guys so much trouble. We'll have to check the times better next time."

"This is unacceptable, Christine." Mrs. Patterson had her arms folded across her chest. "You're grounded."

"Grounded! That's so unfair. You're the ones who drove me there early."

"That's enough, Christine. You had us worried sick."

Mrs. Patterson turned to Peter with a sad look in her eyes. "I'm disappointed in you too, Peter. You should have told us right away. I think maybe it's time you went to your room as well."

Peter couldn't believe that he was in trouble, too. Now, this was really unfair! He knew he should just suck it up, but he'd had enough. "Why should I have to go my room? I didn't do anything!"

"You should have told us right away that you had seen Christine. You saw how worried we were."

Peter couldn't believe this. "I tried to tell you," he said, his eyes bunched together. "None of this is my fault." He knew he was yelling. "I'll go to my room, but only because I want to, not because you told me to. You're not my parents!" Without a glance at anyone, Peter pivoted and ran up to his room. He slammed his door shut. When he saw his books piled on his desk, he threw them on the floor. Then he flopped on his bed. How could Christine have lied like that? And how dare she get him in trouble, too! Peter stared at the ceiling. Any good feelings he had about being in Edmonton were gone. No matter what, he didn't fit in here.

He rolled over and looked at the phone on his desk. He could call his dad and tell him to buy him a plane ticket home. Peter didn't want to stay in Edmonton any longer. He picked up the phone.

Holding the phone in his hand, he thought about the big hockey game that night — the season opener. Peter wanted to play hockey so badly, but to play hockey he had to live here. Peter put down the phone. He'd play his game first, then phone his dad. No matter what, he definitely was going home.

He jumped when he heard a knock on his door.

"Peter," whispered Christine.

He didn't reply.

"Peter, I need to talk to you." She pushed open his door and stepped in, shutting the door behind her. "My parents can't see I'm up here. I'm supposed to be in my room."

"Well go back to your room, then" he muttered.

"I'm sorry." She scrunched up her face.

"Yeah, right."

"No really, I am."

"So?"

"I knew if I made it your fault it would be okay. You're not their kid, so they can't really get too mad at you."

"Well, it's not okay. They did get mad at me. You lied."

"I'll help you with your homework."

"I don't need your help anymore. I'm not going back to school."

"What do you mean?"

"None of your business. Now get out of my room."

After she left, Peter wondered if playing hockey was worth this much agony.

* * *

Mr. Patterson drove Peter to the arena early. The rest of the family had decided to come at game time — Christine, too. She wasn't allowed to go with her friends. She had to sit with the family.

When he got in the car, Peter slouched in his seat and stared out the side window. Mr. Patterson started the car without saying anything and backed out of the driveway.

After ten minutes of silence, Mr. Patterson finally said, "Mrs. Patterson didn't think you should play tonight."

Peter played with his tie. It felt too tight. He never had to wear a tie at home.

"I disagreed with her," continued Mr. Patterson.

"Why?"

"I don't really think much of what happened today was your fault."

"Why did I have to go to my room, then?"

"Reaction. Mrs. Patterson was scared something had happened to Christine. She took it out on you."

"I tried to say something."

"I know that." He winked at Peter. "And I think I convinced my wife of that, too." Mr. Patterson steered the car into the arena parking lot. "Peter, we like having you live with us. And you're a real asset to this hockey team. Don't forget how much you love this game. Things will work out okay at our house." He turned the car off and touched Peter on the shoulder. "I hope you have a good game tonight."

Peter opened his car door, unsure if he even cared if he had a good game. After all, tonight he was phoning his father, and tomorrow he was going home.

In the dressing room, the rest of the team was totally pumped. Peter wanted to feel like everyone else, but everything just seemed so wrong. Tying his laces, he just wanted to get on the ice and skate.

He thought his problems would disappear as usual when he stepped onto the ice, but during warm-up he still felt edgy and tense. He snapped a shot in the top corner and Stu said, "Wow you're on fire. Shoot like that and you'll score."

Peter was on fire all right — but was it the right kind of fire? Everything seemed to be burning out of control.

Peter was put on the first line with Greg and Tanner again. He lined up on his wing, waiting for the ref to drop the puck. He tried to concentrate. *Focus.* The puck dropped.

Tanner slapped the puck back to the defence, so Peter rushed up his wing. He saw the defence from the other team and gritted his teeth. No way was anyone going to hit him. No way was anyone going to take the puck from him. Peter braced his body and slammed the Fort McMurray player into the boards with every ounce of strength. The guy crumpled and fell to the ice. The glass shook and the crowd roared.

Peter picked up the puck and headed to the net. He didn't look for Tanner or Greg. He didn't want to make a pass. Why should he do anyone else a favour? Instead, he glared at the goalie and fired the puck. The Fort McMurray goalie tried to make the save, but the puck zinged past him and into the top corner.

Tanner skated over to Peter and patted him on the back. "Awesome shot, Peter."

Greg joined Tanner and Peter. "Great shot, Peter," he said. "We were open, though."

"So?" said Peter. "You never pass. Why should I pass to you?"

Skating to the bench, Peter didn't feel good about his goal, even when Coach John tapped his helmet.

Next shift out, Peter lined up for the faceoff in the Sherwood Park end. Stu was in his goalie crouch. Peter and Fort McMurray's winger jostled for position. The winger kept trying to cross Peter's stick with his own, to tie him up. It made Peter angry. He braced his legs and shoved his shoulder into the player just as the puck dropped. The player lost his balance and Peter managed to get the puck on the end of his stick. As he was shooting it up the boards, that same winger, now back in the play, tried to check Peter into the boards. Peter swung around and thrust into him again. The whistle blew. The ref pointed to Peter and made the elbowing motion. Penalty.

Fuming, Peter skated to the box. What a dumb call.

When Peter's two minutes were up, Coach John motioned for him to skate to the bench. Why did he have to go to the bench? It was his shift. Peter gulped down some water, waiting for the coach to tell him it was okay, his penalty wasn't really a penalty. But Coach John didn't even talk to Peter.

Peter moved up the line, ready for his next shift. When the Arrows left winger tapped the bench with his stick, Peter was ready to fly. He stepped onto the ice and intercepted a pass. With the puck on the end of his stick, he moved along the boards toward Fort McMurray's end. Out of the corner of his eye, he saw another Arrows player heading toward the net. Should he pass? Peter knew he was skating too deep. He'd never be able to make a decent shot.

Then he saw the Fort McMurray defence coming toward him. He had to pass. Just as Peter batted the puck in the direction of the net, he felt the hit. He crashed against the boards, face first. He felt his blood rush inside of him. He swung around, cross-checking the player who had hit him.

The guy pushed Peter. Peter pushed him back. Another push. And another. Peter couldn't take it any more, so he punched his opponent. The linesman tried to intervene. He felt someone tug on the back of shirt.

"Come on, Peter," said Tanner.

Peter skated away, readjusting his shirt and helmet. The ref made the call. The Fort McMurray player got two minutes for roughing. Peter got two minutes for roughing and two for cross-checking.

"What?" Peter dashed over to the ref. "Why did I get four? He started it. He cross-checked me from behind."

The ref pointed his finger at Peter. "Be quiet or I'll give you a major."

"You don't know how to call a game," yelled Peter. He couldn't stop himself from yelling. He didn't deserve four minutes. The other guy did.

The ref made his motion. Five-minute major for unsportsmanlike conduct.

When he reached the penalty box, Peter threw his stick and gloves before he sat down to take off his helmet.

Now, even hockey sucked.

17

Talk with Coach John

The Sherwood Park Arrows beat the Fort McMurray Blazers 3–2. Peter had scored the first goal, but didn't score again.

At the end of the game, Coach John told Peter to wait for him in the dressing room after everyone had left.

Peter didn't want to talk to the coach. He wanted to go directly to the Pattersons' and phone his dad. He wanted to go home now. Back to the North, where he fit in and nobody insulted him or made him cover for their lies.

He undressed without saying anything to anyone. Dylan, who usually chatted with Peter after every practice, didn't say a word to him. Peter chucked his equipment in his bag, snatched his towel, and went to the showers. He stood under the water for a long time, wanting to hide from everyone. But the hot water didn't wash away the terrible way he felt. Why did they have to ruin hockey, the only thing he loved here?

Finally, he turned the faucet off, re-entered the dressing room, and quietly dressed. Then he sat down and tapped his foot. His stomach ached. If he ran to the toilet to throw up, everyone on the team would talk about him even more. He jiggled his leg. This was horrible. Why didn't everyone leave so he could go, too?

"See you, Peter," said Dylan softly.

Peter shrugged. *Maybe, maybe not.* If he left, he wouldn't see any of these people ever again.

After every player was gone and Peter was alone in the dressing room, Coach John entered.

"Peter," he said. "I think we need a chat."

Peter stared at the floor. He felt Coach John sit down beside him.

"You took a lot of penalties tonight."

Peter kept staring at the floor.

"Why?"

"I dunno."

"Are you angry at something?"

"I don't like it here."

"I understand how hard this must be for you. But you're a great hockey player and have a future in this game. Today should be a learning experience for you. You can't hold everything inside and then let bad feelings out with bad play. Carrying outside anger onto the ice doesn't help your game." He paused. "Peter, look at me."

His hair sticking to his face, Peter slowly looked up. Coach John tilted his head and said, "I believe in you, Peter. I believe you can fulfill your dream. And I'll do anything I can to help, but *you* have to want this."

"I do want to play hockey, but …"

"But what, Peter?"

"I … miss my family so much. And my home. It's just so different here."

Coach John put his hand on Peter's shoulder. "I know. It's good to miss your friends and family. It means you love them and that they love you. Your home will always be there for you, you know. It won't go away."

"I wish my dad …" Peter's voice cracked.

"I called your dad after the game."

"You did?" said Peter, surprised.

"He thinks he might bring your sister to come watch a game soon. I have some extra airline credits he can use for one of the tickets. He wants you to call him tonight when you get back to the Pattersons'." Coach John patted Peter's knee. "And I set up an exhibition game today with a Calgary team. I think you have a friend on that team — Josh Watson."

"We're going to play Josh's team? Really?"

"Yeah, really."

"I also talked to your teacher yesterday."

Peter stared at the floor.

"She says you're doing okay, but it looks as if you may need some extra help. My wife used to be a teacher and she's tutored a few of my players in the past. How about we set something up with her?" He paused. "We can make this work, Peter — if you want it to."

Peter didn't reply.

* * *

Out in the arena lobby, Peter saw the Patterson family standing by themselves by the bulletin board. They probably thought he was the worst hockey player in the world right now. Mr. Patterson stepped forward when Peter walked over. "You want a drink, Peter?"

"Nah, it's okay." He quickly glanced at Christine. Her face was all red and her eyes looked puffy. She was probably upset because she couldn't sit with her friends.

The air outside was fresh and Peter sucked in a deep breath. He pulled his bag over to Mr. Patterson's car. The rest of the Patterson family followed. Why didn't they go to Mrs. Patterson's van?

Mr. Patterson popped the trunk, and Peter threw his bag in and shut the trunk. When he turned, Christine stood beside him, wringing her hands.

"Go ahead, Christine," said Mr. Patterson.

"I'm so sorry I lied about you, Peter."

Peter looked at Mrs. Patterson. She nodded her head at Christine. "Keep talking, honey."

"I know I got you into trouble and it wasn't your fault. And then you got all those penalties." She wiped the tears off her face. "I was the one not being a good sport."

"It's okay," he muttered. Why did she have to cry?

"No, it's not okay," said Mrs. Patterson. "I'm sorry too, Peter. I misjudged the situation. Maybe I should have received a penalty for unsportsmanlike conduct." She smiled sadly at him. "You know, we like having you live with us, Peter."

Christine shoved her hands in her jeans pockets. "If you'll let me, I'll make it up to you. I can continue helping you with your homework. And I promise I won't make any more deals. I'm grounded for the next few weeks, so I have to be at home anyway."

"I think Coach John is going to get someone else to help me. That is, if I stay."

Christine scrunched up her face. "You're not going to go home because of me, are you?"

Peter shrugged.

"You can't go home," said Christine. "You're, like, the best hockey player on your team."

"And who will play mini-sticks with me?" Andrew asked.

"Peter can do whatever he wants," said Mr. Patterson, patting Peter on the back. "This is his decision to make."

18

Big Decision

The ride home was super quiet. Peter didn't say too much and oddly enough neither did Mr. Patterson. As he steered the car into the driveway, Mr. Patterson said, "You know, Peter, you can phone home as often as you like. We have a great phone plan that covers your calls."

"Okay," said Peter.

"If you do stay, I think you might be wise to get help from Coach John's wife. It might make it easier for you. Christine has good intentions and is a good student, but I think you're better with someone outside our house."

"Yeah."

"And, Peter," Mr. Patterson paused and Peter finally looked up, "you can talk to me if things are bothering you. If you share what's bothering you, it doesn't take control and make you take bad penalties."

Inside the house, Peter went up to his room. He sat at the desk and picked up the phone. For a moment he sat there, just listening to the dial tone. Then he took a deep breath and punched in the numbers. His dad answered after the first ring.

"Peter, we've been waiting for your call."

"Hi, Dad."

"I talked to your coach earlier. I guess you had a tough game."

"Yeah. I got lots of penalties."

"I heard."

Silence.

"Is everything okay?"

"I guess."

More silence.

"What's going on, Pete?"

"I dunno. I want to play hockey, but I want to come home, too."

"Why? What's wrong?"

"It's so different here."

"Pete, you'll always have your home here. But there's no guarantee hockey will be there for you if you give it up."

"I know, but it's so hard to live here."

"How about trying to stick it out until Christmas?"

"Christmas? That's still three months away."

"You have a lot of games between now and then. If hockey is something you really want to do, then you should try to stay in Edmonton. If you really want to come home then that's okay, too. But don't just run away because a few things aren't working out so well." When Peter didn't answer, he went on. "Susie and I might come down. Would that help things?"

"Yeah." Peter twisted the telephone cord. "When would you come?"

"How about near the end of October? That's just four weeks away."

"We could take Susie to the mall."

"She's standing right here. Do you want to talk to her?"

"Sure."

"Hi, Peter," said Susie. "Don't give up, okay? I know you love hockey."

"How come you don't e-mail me any more?" he asked.

"I still e-mail."

"Not every day." Peter missed bantering with Susie.

"Okay," she said in her big-sister voice. "I promise to e-mail every day if you promise not to give up."

"You promise? I'm going to hold you to this," said Peter, smiling.

"Yeah," she said. She paused. Then she softly said, "We miss you tons, but you were born to play hockey. It's in your blood and nothing you do can take it out. Just like you and me, we're blood, too. Nothing will ever change that. So you have to play. Don't quit okay? I want to watch you play in the NHL one day and be able to say, 'That's my brother.'"

Peter laughed. Susie was his biggest fan.

When Peter hung up the phone, he knew Susie was right — hockey was in his blood. He went to his closet and pulled out his drum. His home and his culture were in his blood, too. He didn't have to live there to stay connected to everyone. It was up to him. He'd give this another try and stay in Edmonton till Christmas at least.

He drummed his fingers on the caribou hide and started to sing.

Other books you'll enjoy in the Sports Stories series

Baseball

❏ *Curve Ball* by John Danakas #1
Tom Poulos is looking forward to a summer of baseball in Toronto until his mother puts him on a plane to Winnipeg.

❏ *Baseball Crazy* by Martyn Godfrey #10
Rob Carter wins an all-expenses-paid chance to be bat boy at the Blue Jays spring training camp in Florida.

❏ *Slam Dunk* by Steven Barwin #23
The Raptors are going co-ed, but Mason and his friends aren't sure how they feel about it.

❏ *Shark Attack* by Judi Peers #25
The East City Sharks have a good chance of winning the county championship until their arch rivals get a tough new pitcher.

❏ *Courage on the Line* by Cynthia Bates #33
Amelie seems like a happy-go-lucky twelve year old. So why is she having nightmares and why did she change schools midway through the year?

❏ *Hit and Run* by Dawn Hunter and Karen Hunter #35
Glen Thomson is a talented pitcher, but as his ego inflates, team morale plummets. Will he learn from being benched for losing his temper?

❏ *Power Hitter* by C. A. Forsyth #41
Connor's summer was looking like a write-off. That is, until he discovered his secret talent.

❏ *Sayonara, Sharks* by Judi Peers #48
In this sequel to *Shark Attack*, Ben and Kate are excited about the school trip to Japan, but Matt's not sure he wants to go.

❏ *Out of Bounds* by Sylvia Gunnery # 70
When the Hirtle family's house burns down, Jay is forced to relocate and switch schools. He has a choice: sacrifice a year of basketball or play on the same team as his arch-rival Mike.

Basketball

❑ *Fast Break* by Michael Coldwell #8
Moving from Toronto to small-town Nova Scotia was rough, but when Jeff makes the school basketball team he thinks things are looking up.

❑ *Camp All-Star* by Michael Coldwell #12
In this insider's view of a basketball camp, Jeff Lang encounters some unexpected challenges.

❑ *Nothing but Net* by Michael Coldwell #18
The Cape Breton Grizzly Bears prepare for an out-of-town basketball tournament they're sure to lose.

❑ *Slam Dunk* by Steven Barwin and Gabriel David Tick #23
In this sequel to *Roller Hockey Blues*, Mason Ashbury's basketball team adjusts to the arrival of some new players: girls.

❑ *Courage on the Line* by Cynthia Bates #33
After Amelie changes schools, she must confront difficult former team-mates in an extramural match.

❑ *Free Throw* by Jacqueline Guest #34
Matthew Eagletail must adjust to a new school, a new team and a new father along with five pesky sisters.

❑ *Triple Threat* by Jacqueline Guest #38
Matthew's cyber-pal Free Throw comes to visit, and together they face a bully on the court.

❑ *Queen of the Court* by Michele Martin Bossley #40
What happens when the school's fashion queen winds up on the basket-ball court?

❑ *Shooting Star* by Cynthia Bates #46
Quyen is dealing with a troublesome teammate on her new basketball team, as well as trouble at home. Her parents seem haunted by something that happened in Vietnam.

❑ *Home Court Advantage* by Sandra Diersch #51
Debbie had given up hope of being adopted, until the Lowells came along.

Things were looking up, until Debbie is accused of stealing from the team.

❏ *Rebound* by Adrienne Mercer #54
C.J.'s dream in life is to play on the national basketball team. But one day she wakes up in pain and can barely move her joints, much less be a star player.

❏ *Out of Bounds* by Gunnery Sylvia #70
Jay must switch schools after a house fire. He must either give up the basketball season or play alongside his rival at his new school.

Ice Hockey

❏ *Two Minutes for Roughing* by Joseph Romain #2
As a new player on a tough Toronto hockey team, Les must fight to fit in.

❏ *Hockey Night in Transcona* by John Danakas #7
Cody Powell gets promoted to the Transcona Sharks' first line, bumping out the coach's son, who's not happy with the change.

❏ *Face Off* by C. A. Forsyth #13
A talented hockey player finds himself competing with his best friend for a spot on a select team.

❏ *Hat Trick* by Jacqueline Guest #20
The only girl on an all-boy hockey team works to earn the captain's respect and her mother's approval.

❏ *Hockey Heroes* by John Danakas #22
A left-winger on the thirteen-year-old Transcona Sharks adjusts to a new best friend and his mom's boyfriend.

❏ *Hockey Heat Wave* by C. A. Forsyth #27
In this sequel to *Face Off*, Zack and Mitch run into trouble when it looks as if only one of them will make the select team at hockey camp.

❏ *Shoot to Score* by Sandra Richmond #31
Playing defense on the B list alongside the coach's mean-spirited son is a tough obstacle for Steven to overcome, but he perseveres and changes his luck.

one diabetes is working against him — and getting more serious by the day.

❏ *Deflection! by Bill Swan #71*
Justin and his two best friends play road hockey together and are members of the same league team. But some personal rivalries and interference from Justin's three all-too-supportive grandfathers start to create tension among the players.

❏ *Misconduct* by Beverly Scudamore #72
Matthew has always been a popular student and hockey player. But after an altercation with a tough kid named Dillon at hockey camp, Matt finds himself number one on the bully's hit list.

Roughing by Lorna Schultz Nicholson #74
Josh is off to an elite hockey camp for the summer, where his roommate, Peter, is skilled enough to give Kevin, the star junior player, some serious competition, creating trouble on and off the ice.

❏ *Home Ice* by Beatrice Vandervelde #76
Leigh Aberdeen is determined to win the hockey championship with a new, all girls team, the Chinooks.

❏ *Against the Boards* by Lorna Schultz Nicholson #77
Peter has made it onto an AAA Bantam team and is now playing hockey in Edmonton. But this shy boy from the Northwest Territories is having a hard time adjusting to his new life.

Roller Hockey

❏ *Roller Hockey Blues* by Steven Barwin and Gabriel David Tick #17
Mason Ashbury faces a summer of boredom until he makes the roller hockey team.

Running

❏ *Fast Finish* by Bill Swan #30
Noah is a promising young runner headed for the provincial finals when he suddenly decides to withdraw from the event.